DATE DUE			
Oct 15 69.			

GAYLORD M-2   PRINTED IN U.S.A.

THE GOGGLERS

" In a few seconds no covering remained around his crotch, and the measuring, by both men and women, made him so standupish that some stood back in awe."

THE GOGGLERS

A Political Satire

by EDWARD RAIDEN

Published by

SATURN BOOKS

Los Angeles, California

THE GOGGLERS
Copyright © 1967 by
EDWARD RAIDEN

Library of Congress Catalog Card No. 67-29388

PRINTED IN UNITED STATES OF AMERICA BY
Theo. Gaus' Sons, Inc., BROOKLYN, N. Y.

Part I
LONGFELLOW

FOR DAYS AND DAYS Longfellow had tossed about with the space capsule. Braced against the side, he gazed hopelessly around into space. His six feet looked taller, and his gaunt face lined by worry framing the deeply sunken eyes, made his broad nose appear extremely flat from behind the coverage of his helmet. The space suit bulged about him like a fat scarecrow. There was still some food left but the water was almost gone. He glanced ruefully at the frayed parachute fixed to the small mast outside.

With no idea of which heaven he was in, he was suddenly conscious of a queer notion, induced by an odd shimmy of his crib, that if he had a grappling line to shoot out it would grab on to something. Smiling faintly at the absurdity of the idea, he bent forward to tighten the lashings which held him. Just then the capsule lurched wildly under him, and a crashing shock split it in two, wrenched him from his hold and pitched him forward like a ball. As he hurtled through the air, he grasped madly at emptiness. In a stunning second the small pod in space had become a place of safety. His mind flashed a picture he had once seen . . . a man alone thrashing wildly about, shouting desperately at a disappearing horizon.

Within a second of being catapulted out of the crib's rotating hips, Longfellow felt the sensation of his suit catching and ripping on sharp points that raked his arms and legs—and then a hard landing. While he lay where he had landed, semi-conscious, trying to focus his eyes to see around him and trying to concentrate to shut off the whining dynamo in his ears and head, he felt himself beset by many hands, exploring and measuring him; and the hands tore away at the suit where it interfered with free handling and examination.

In a few seconds no covering remained around his crotch, and the measuring, by both men and women, made him so standupish that some stood back in awe. Mouths agape, eyes shifting from their measuring implements to the object of their measuring, and back again to their measuring implements, they stood in arrested tableau, gaping, gawking and goggling, held posed by the object of their admiration. Others, shocked or not, continued to ply their instruments of measure around, along and from root to tip of Longfellow's connection with the past and future.

This was most unusual. Where he came from, when you land they examine your clothes, the food and liquor you are carrying, your antecedents, and finally you. Longfellow knew as a student of government, that examinations were necessary, but this method was all wrong. Law is founded on reason, he thought. What should be the law—is the law. Or was it—what is the law—should be the law? He couldn't remember the exact quotation. His instinctive resistance to the invasion of his privacy was just so much unreasoned opposition to the law of the land. He ceased his resistance. The torn remnants of a magnificent space suit were almost completely gone by the time a voice of authority penetrated his consciousness and that of the crowd.

"Away, away. Not see he be strange and not candidate?"

The crowd fell back and Longfellow, dazed and dumbfounded, bruised and badly shaken, looked around at the people. They looked like others he knew but they were different. He concentrated and then it penetrated. They were all models of the museum model of the Neanderthal man which he had seen, but the skin of some of them was smooth and clean shaven while that of others was hairy, in tufts, knots and tassels; the clothing of the people was quite different from what he was used to, for those portions of the body which he had always seen uncovered were in their case covered, and organs which he had always seen covered were exposed. It was very confusing, for the law under which he had lived condemned the exposure of what he now saw and permitted exposure of areas here covered.

The nearest man wore a hat, and a jacket so short that the bare skin of the stomach was visible. Underneath, his shirt left a space around the stomach exposed although it covered the shoulders, chest and back. Longfellow was quite startled to note that the pants unveiled the link between generations—always hidden in his country—except in the performance of its functions, and even then frequently covered or used surreptitiously. When the man turned, the rear section of his pants was cut out to form an amusing parenthesis around his buttocks. The garment was a filagree exposing the middle, stomach, crotch and thighs, and the pants, or so they appeared to be, covered the rest of the legs and the outer side of the thighs.

Were these clothes thought Longfellow? Nearby a woman wore a dress that covered one bosom, revealing the other, a white mound sealed with a brown cap and the rest of her dress not connected to the upper part, was a diaper shaped cloth. When she turned, a quick glance showed Longfellow that the buttocks had been barbered.

All of these observations took but a few moments. Then Longfellow burst into incoherent speech and his benefactor smiled and spoke gently. "Take ease. I be Doctor. Thee in haven. All be right and order. Thee be all right." The man's jaw rotated as he explained, and Longfellow watched the chin make orbits that barely missed his nose and chest. "People understood not position. Thee be on back, on ground, and it be nigh to period of select for Gogg. These did think thee be candidate."

Longfellow looked at this creature who called himself a doctor, uncomprehending, and then before the doctor could clarify, began jerking out words that were both questions and arguments.

"My capsule! The sky! All changed into a street," he snapped his fingers in disbelief, "like that! Please," he leaned forward and grasped the doctor's arm, "tell me; is this another world? Am I dead? Please . . . I must know the truth."

"Hold on friend. Ease self. I now did tell thee be safe." The doctor took Longfellow's hand and helped him to stand. "Thee be on Planet in sky."

Longfellow's voice sounded incredulous. He looked desperate. "A Planet? But there wasn't a cloud in the sky for the three weeks I was floating out of orbit. I was watching the horizon and there was never a sign of a meteor or any heavenly body. A second before the crash the horizon was clear, ceiling unlimited, and not a speck of dust in sight."

Leaning back on his heels he said with resignation, "I had a wild notion that I could touch something if I reached out; I knew I was getting flight mirages. Now I know I'm hallucinating. None of this is real. I must be dreaming."

The doctor patted his arm reassuringly. "Calm. Thee normal and these incident explain in nature, in spite of shock. Be on Goggle . . . not on mirage. Atmosphere gross intense. Eye in space see not image. Eye on Goggle, see not space. Expect thee find simple race, simple manner and idea."

Longfellow stole a look at his professional adviser. His clothes were quite what earth would expect from a doctor for they covered him completely. However, the face gave him pause. There was something underslung about the jaw and when its owner talked, it rotated and moved up and down like that of an old man without teeth, even though this man was obviously not old. The rest of the face was flat. The eyes, with tiny pupils like single dots on a pair of dice, were set back and wide apart, separated by a broad, flat nose.

The doctor beckoned to Longfellow and moved ahead with the rolling gait of an ape, suspending extremely long arms. Noticing the general appearance of things reminded Longfellow he was in a strange place and he must find out about getting home. He followed along.

"How are your contacts with the outside world?"

"Outside world? Thy world?"

4

Longfellow nodded.

"We not contact with outside world. Before, once Goggle receive man from people out space." He smiled and drew a deep breath that made his chest stand out. "Direct forbear." His eyes became dreamy, the tiny points rolling upward in reverent recollection. "Great man. Father of country, be call here." Suddenly he turned to Longfellow and placed his arm around his shoulders. "And so be with thee except thee be dark. People not realize thee be purebred foreign or would acclaim. Thee have much to give Goggle in develop. Thee too be of advance breed and civilize."

As they walked along Longfellow observed the people and the surroundings. He was distracted by a woman who passed by. Below the waist she wore the same loin cloth garment which he had seen on the other woman, but, above the waistline, her dress draped across both shoulders and left both breasts exposed.

Was there a pattern here, he wondered, as his eyes followed the woman's lumbering gait that rippled the muscles of her buttocks. This woman, these women that he saw, and those at home —there was a striking difference and yet they were the same. A little variation in the features, less variety in the physiognomy, an oddity in the form. Strange to him, yet they were not all strange. The doctor spoke his language. How could these people be so like him and like everything he knew, and still be so strange and different from everything he knew? Turning to the doctor with all of this to ask Longfellow saw that the doctor had anticipated him.

"Thee land from out space to here and wish understand how, why, where, when, and much else. Make demand all one. Come to house and as possible without addle thee, answer all question. Exchange, inform most easy and pleasure. Assure not more remarkable than cast on Planet not enjoy intercourse with thy people. Fill belly and talk all question now confuse mind and eye."

"But you are civilized people. Don't you have contact with the outside world?" Longfellow expected a negative answer.

"Civilize true. But not contact."

"You are civilized and any such people would seek to contact the outside world." He held his breath, waiting for a ray of hope

5

—for word of the possibility that he might return to his own world. The doctor had no solace for him.

"Ah, Sire, thee do misjudge. Here have small thing, but not advance. Other civilize far ahead and we copy. Proud indeed such culture as thy, and shame we backward. Be confine to Planet . . . Be Goggler; proud of land; but only Goggler."

"But your intelligence! Your natural aptitude! And your need for growth and progress!" argued Longfellow.

"Thee right. But be simple race. Most great of civilize be thy own. Follow form of govern laid for we but not refine . . . Sire. There be drawback . . . imagine govern refine to separate of hair by most high develop and rationalize mind."

Longfellow looked at him skeptically. He found it difficult to understand the doctor, who finished off, "Imagine simple approach to matter require subtle?"

Impatient with the doctor's failure to answer his questions about the chances of getting off the Planet, Longfellow's voice betrayed signs of irritation. "Is it possible for me to obtain equipment and build a capsule?"

"Not. Have not material; have not such builder."

"No builder? I could build it myself; put together the force for blastoff. How about explosives? Do you have any?"

"Not. Have not explosive. Soil volcanic and not have machine."

"Then I'm a prisoner!"

"Not. Why say? Thee be free. Reception most great when people realize who be. Be receive as new Great."

Longfellow walked along in silence, reflecting on his fate. His space capsule had landed in another world. The name of the place was Goggle. These primitive people had somehow learned the English language, albeit in a primitive form. There was enough communication for him to be able to learn more about them, to learn more about his position, and to learn exactly what his status with them would be. These questions were most important to him at this moment, for the permanence of his exile bore in upon him.

Every few seconds the doctor glanced over to him but found

"Set back many feet from the walk, the doctor's home was excavated from the stone, spiraling upward unevenly and bent to finish in a point like a ram's horn. Large grounds spun in circles surrounding it."

him absorbed in his thoughts. Suddenly the doctor exclaimed, "My Gogg! We in square of house and never realize!"

Longfellow looked around. Busy with his own thoughts, he hadn't observed the things they had passed. The fall, the walk, had made everything hazy. He was vaguely aware of stone structures and stone paved streets. Now, for the first time really seeing, he looked around. He found a street which might have been in the suburb of any city back on earth. Everything appeared to be of stone, and those in the road formed a design in whorls, with no indication where they began or ended. Rather, they seemed spun right through. Whoever made the design had traveled in circles, paying close followers with dizziness. Set back many feet from the walk, the doctor's home was excavated from the stone, spiraling upward unevenly and bent to finish in a point like a ram's horn. Large grounds spun in circles surrounding it.

Like a little boy in wonderment, Longfellow followed the doctor, making the turns of the walk down into the house. The two were met by a servant who resembled an ape more than any of the other Gogglers he had seen. The servant's suit covered his body completely and although they were inside the doorway, he also wore a hat which he did not remove. The greeting, intended to convey complete obeisance, surprised Longfellow, as the servant, without touching the ground with his hands did a complete somersault, landing on his feet in the spot from which he had sprung, facing them as if he had not moved.

"Bulbo, give friend towel fresh and clothes mine, and show room."

Bulbo gazed at Longfellow blankly, shrugged so his body raised upward, raising eyebrows, shoulders and hips, and shook his head up and down and from side to side in a bewildering manner. Then in acknowledgment of his lower status Bulbo bent forward and backed out, head down and arms hanging so they almost touched the floor. Longfellow followed. He found the servant's padding side to side walk like that of the rocking of a boat.

The guestroom style was strange and new to Longfellow also, for it was bald from floor to ceiling in a flat white color, and round like the cupola of an old fashioned castle. For a second

8

"The greeting, intended to complete obeisance, surprised Longfellow, as the servant, without touching the ground with his hands did a complete somersault, landing on his feet in the spot from which he had sprung."

Longfellow thought he was in a pill-box. The furniture, a simple and severely dressed single bed, a white chair carved out of one solid piece, and a dresser with holes instead of drawers, suggested some of the abstract or surrealist pieces and paintings Longfellow had seen, with little relationship to time, period or design. They might have been carved pieces or just the odd result of volcanic stone falling in a mould. The thought made him smile as he visualized a volcano belching chairs and dressers and beds of lava. Relieved to discover the counterpane was cloth, he sat on the edge of the bed to remove what was left of his space outfit.

As he undressed, Bulbo brought towels and clothes, and Longfellow washed in the lava-made sink into which water was poured from a standing pitcher. The plumbing facilities were no more than holes through which the water ran off when the stoppers were removed. Refreshed by the washing, he put on the doctor's clothes and walked up and down the room, stopping several times to survey himself. The clothes fit him in odd spots, but not in others. He looked in the pockets for a quartermaster's label, sure that only the GI services could misfit a fellow so completely. With his hands he grasped the cloth in the chest where there was enough extra for a full blown female. The sleeves hung over his hands like those of a Chinese Kimono, and the trousers had seat enough for him to bend or bow without wrinkling the suit. At the same time, where there was seemingly ample cloth, there was a strain against the inside of his knees, as though the pants insisted on putting him in shape to ride a horse.

As he looked at himself he realized that under the circumstances this kind of criticism was a cock-eyed point of view. He'd had a rough time of it. Never did he expect rescue and now that he had found a haven, he was questioning that haven. If the future was doubtful, at least he could be grateful that there was a future. What, after all, was home and life, but the immediate vision and what fancy did with the past? His rescue, or fate, if it was not rescue, still lay before him. Was he a fatalist, accepting what transpired or threatened, only when all was bleak and hopeless? And when he found far more than he had said he hoped for, was he unwilling to put up with fate? Was he a trigger-happy

"The thought made him smile as he visualized a volcano belching chairs and dressers and beds of lava."

pilot who started shooting before the enemy was in range, or before there was an enemy? No. His training must stand with him. Don't turn on the fire 'til there's something to cook. With shoulders back, and chin in, he put his chest out and said "I am the military."

Downstairs he found his host seated in an armchair. The doctor raised his eyes as Longfellow entered.

"Ah. Thee look to home. Forget old country and be we." He indicated a chair nearby formed like a nest, made of a grey volcanic stone. "Sit please. Food soon be."

"Thank you." The sides of the chair Longfellow sat in reached to his shoulders. His hands scraped against a rough pumice-like surface. "I trust it will not offend you if I ask questions about you, your people and your land."

The doctor was delighted.

"See? More high develop culture take turn and deviate which simple Goggler not take. Because simple, ask abrupt for inform." He continued. "But, aside nice manner thee understand, ask what ever. Any."

Longfellow, slow to take up from there, found the calm of the doctor and the serenity of the household encouraging.

"You said you would tell me all about your land and its people. Of course, I mean no offense, but the clothes the people wear, they . . . they reveal so much. Is that usual?"

"Ah yes. Be intend."

"Intended? Isn't that a little surprising?"

"Not. Be proud of what show."

"Oh?"

"Let explain. People once early men tribe. Of course," he hurried to explain, "long back. But much hundred year, man like Sire be jump on Goggle. Be only other thy race, as did I tell before, who be here. First man we ever see. First sign of civilize; first sample culture people ever know. Rub civilize person long, some culture sure come off; and come off, it attach in part to person who rub. Man . . . name Peter . . . be symbol of civilize and culture and progress. Peter Father of Country. Visit female and offspring be less hair and less animal, and people understand change for culture and civilize. Acclaim and seek Peter help make all better; with cooperate all become assimmolate and more culture. Any oppose, deliberate retard progress and be enemy of people. Peter acclaim by all and all seek civilize offspring.

"Cooperate of Peter be main part life . . . be assimmolate . . . be obvious more pure strain be more great culture and civilize. For quick develop, Peter breed offspring to many generation. I, for instance," he said it very proudly, "be purebred. Purebred as could, because forebear, up to many great-great-grandfather be all sire by Peter . . . 'til he die."

"That's very interesting," said Longfellow, "but . . . oh," he added, the light of realization suddenly breaking in on him, "that's why the people looked so . . . ah, ah, ... unusual to me. Faces were flat and jaws underslung. Not yours, of course."

"No, I far more better than other. Be why doctor. Now thee purify strain more. Dark skin more interest. Increase civilize. Wait 'til see wife. I love," he said, rubbing his hands and walking up and down the room excitedly, "have child most pure culture and most great civilize."

Longfellow looked at him rather doubtfully and said, "But all of that hardly explains the clothes. The people wear such unusual clothes. They expose parts of their bodies which where I come from are kept hidden."

"That?" said the doctor. "Be easy explain. Thy people be similar and not show identity by clothes. Peter say wear clothes which display advance. People proud of more great culture and civilize and show be descend from Great Peter. What be evident of increment of culture and civilize?"

For a moment the doctor stopped and then continued. "Only evident by physical resemble Peter. Most outstand about Peter," he suddenly interrupted his trend of thought and asked, "By chance, what be name?"

"Peter Longfellow."

"Splendid! Splendid!" He sat down stunned, face bright with exaltation; and in an instant reaction stood up and marched about the room triumphantly as he rejoiced. "Thee pronounce different, but be same and be direct inherit of title of Peter and all thing revere on Goggle." Just as abruptly as he had shifted his direction of thinking, he shifted back again. "Most distinguish quality Peter . . . must call Peter One . . . be that skin, except for few place, had not hair. Mature Goggler have hair all over. First child of Peter One show sign of less hair, be proof of connect with Great Peter; and proof of culture and civilize. Since be proud of proof, what more nature than wear clothes which cover part of body which have hair and keep hide animal descend? Same time, clothes puff importance and show off culture and civilize by leave uncover part of body which not have hair. Some fraud shave, but we alway can detect affectation as low conduct of low people; people with pretend to show off as more high caste."

"That," said Longfellow, "seems quite reasonable and plausible. Naturally," he added, "Peter One designed the garment. Ah . . . mmmmm . . . the clothes your people wore before the change in their manners, customs, and culture, what were they?"

"Clothes? Goggler be beast before come culture. No clothes . . . no culture . . . no pride . . . no civilize." The doctor seemed anxious to hurry on with his discussion of history.

"Natural Peter One design garment after garment of same name . . . cuirass and breastplate. As do thee know, lower garment be cuirass. Peter One carry over name from garment which familiar to he."

Longfellow recalled that the cuirass and breastplate had been in use in Europe during the Middle Ages and on down through the Eighteenth century, and the impudent misapplication of names to the present garments, and the entire set of circumstances suggested that Peter One had had an evil sense of humor. Even more was this so since Peter One was the only one who could see the humor in the situations he had created. The Gogglers, it was clear, had taken everything seriously.

"What are the names for women's clothes? The cuirass is the lower garment for men, you say. Is that the name for women's lower garments as well?"

"Certain. Be not different name garment for men or women.

After all," the doctor smiled deprecatingly, assured that with this statement there could be no disagreement, "clothes have not sex."

"No," repeated Longfellow, thinking about all the movies he had seen and the women he'd met.

"What," he inquired a moment later, "is the name of your women's upper garment?" One from two left one, but he wanted the doctor to repeat it.

"Be breastplate. Simple, not?"

"Yes. Very simple. Of course, Peter One supplied that?"

Something in Longfellow's manner and voice made the doctor suspicious. "Yes. Peter One supply name, as already I tell. Why? Be some wrong?"

"Wrong? Certainly not. It's perfect." He passed from the subject by referring to another. "That explains the clothes naming situation perfectly but if I recall . . . of course, I may have been confused . . . it struck me that one of the first women I saw was wearing no breastplate at all. No, wait a minute, she was wearing a breastplate but it exposed one breast. While another woman I saw was wearing no breastplate at all, unless the cloth around her shoulders, which left exposed her two breasts, could be called a breastplate. Are there such differences in style?"

"Ah yes. Be decide different style . . . by caste and practice display of what one have. Still follow pride of descend from Peter One, women show breast because culture and civilize. To have breast mean blood of Peter. And most breast be with less hair and Goggler love display all part of body which be with less or no hair."

Continuing, the doctor said, "Peter One set up caste. In course of descend, assimmolation, some have more Peter and some less. These with more be more culture and more civilize. These more close with Peter One. More great . . . civilize of course . . . more great breast. Most endow have two. Most far remove from ancestry of civilize, least assimmolate, be less culture and less other attribute of Peter. First woman thee see have first cross, half Peter and half Goggler. Be why have one breast."

The doctor halted, reached for what looked like a cigar, lit it and waited a few moments. Longfellow turned his mind to the

15

skidding comedy-scenario that Peter One had composed, visualizing him plucking a string here and striking a chord there, all the while grinning and grimacing, and playing the dual role of Pan and Pandora. The doctor resumed, his voice a trifle weary.

"There be other, thee not see, who be most far remove from Peter, most far remove from culture and civilize, not yet assimmolate. These have nothing. Add great misfortune, when be without breast, be flat-chest and when flat chest, be hairy, and flat chest and hairy, do try to hide fact by wear special breastplate. Such be beautiful and deceive . . . but good judge tell true culture and true descend or just boast. Wearer hope critic not examine close and see fraud. Proverb say, not matter how beautiful breastplate, woman be false and shame of lack of assimmolate and inherit and culture from Peter."

"Do you have titles to distinguish between the castes?"

"Definite and most right so. These with less of Peter be most low caste called No-Peter."

"No-Peter? You mean they have no descent from Peter One?"

"Not precise. History teach Peter One be forebear to all, but early time divide and one group continue assimmolate and other group not continue. Divide be politic . . . some radical . . . some conservative. High caste . . . two divide in line of descend . . . those assimmolate with most Peter endow of culture and civilize be call Peters."

The arrangements of the past could be confounding, Longfellow supposed, unless they were one's own. Simplicity was easier to come by if you could just toss away an idea or a plan when it didn't work out and you were the last word. Toss out and start again. Giving attention to the doctor and complimenting him to stir the flow of history, Longfellow said, "There is a finesse in the cleavage between the different classes. Women where I come from are also proud of this heritage. In different ways, they also display that pride."

"Be so? Be wonderful!"

"Wonderful? Why wonderful?"

"Because happen here. If happen thy people, Goggler be more and more civilize, more and more like Peter."

The doctor leaned over toward Longfellow with great animation and added, "woman be proud of descend from Peter and show proof forthright. Result she be admire and envy by crowd. Women with not wonderful develop Peter give, use breastplate make believe do have. Breastplate some big in breast, some stand like statue, some point breast, some make breast tight but full, and some flat as though hide. None so interest and attract as assimmolate from Peter."

From his first struggling experience Longfellow had wondered why the people measured his penis when he was prostrate. Other notions and other questions had run through his mind, the many new impressions and symbols playing hide and seek with his curiosity. But the scene of the explorations of the Gogglers who invaded his privacy when they were measuring his . . . he found it difficult to use the word penis, for since he was a child it had been a taboo word, his mother substituting the word ting-a-ling and he following suit whenever there had been occasion to refer to it—and now he found it easier, even in thinking of it, to think of it as his . . . ting-a-ling while he was lying on the paving stones had recurred to him several times, and he was sure they must have meaning. The incident now goaded his intention to ask enlargement of the doctor's few words of explanation.

"Tell me Doctor, you suggested that when I first landed the people seized . . . err, well, examined my (he couldn't say ting-a-ling out loud to a strange man, or any man for that matter) . . . penis because they thought I was a political candidate. Now you say that the voter measures a candidate for Gogg. What do you mean? What is the Gogg?"

Longfellow sat in ambush for some new and malicious ribaldry conceived by his predecessor, Peter.

"Mean? Why Gogg be Chief of govern; and, we be democrazy, all, from low to high, from No-Peter to Peter, have same right to vote choose of Gogg."

"What is the general system? What is the manner and basis for election?"

"Take moment, Sire. These be many thing. Let take first question. Govern. Be democrazy. First thing Peter One insist be demo-

crazy. Democrazy be voice of most great number, and people, be
. . . well, if not savage, at least not train, not know how govern
self or have democrazy."

"What did they do? Can you explain?"

The doctor's tone was disparaging. "On Goggle, Chief of govern be head, chose by popular choose . . . fundamental custom."

Betraying by his quizzical look his failure to understand what
the doctor was explaining, Longfellow's reaction caused the doctor to hold his hand up.

"In minute . . . not rush." After a pause he added, "most big
on Goggle be Gogg."

Peter looked inquiringly at the doctor. "You mean that when
I was thrown on Goggle, and all the people started to pull at me
before you called them off, they thought I was a candidate for
Gogg and they were measuring my penis for that purpose?"

"Exact," said the doctor, brightening. "Be exact what happen.
Well understand! Perhaps did notice when say, 'Be not candidate,' these did desist."

"That's your theory of democracy? That's more like the
divine right of kings. A man inherits the size of his sexual organ,
so that with it he would inherit the Goggship. That would not be
democratic."

"Oh? Be evolution of govern in democrazy." The doctor
settled back as he explained.

"When Goggle first inhabit, before record, as in all tribe of
animal, select be most big. Usual most strong. Goggler manage
agree who most big because always he prove point. First Gogg
be choose 'til too old. When Peter One come and control, he say
Gogg be who most big, not most strong. He explain care of office
require fearless understand. Care of office wear down incumbent
and he hold long after able. People follow Peter One wisdome,
agree Gogg be select because most big.

"Period of measure for select and discuss of measure with
free opine among Goggler necessary. Real test be relative. At
meet of ten, one more important than at meet of ten thousand.
By compare with other, tell which most big.

"Period of five month, when people measure applicant, try

all, and choose most big. End period, new Gogg be select. Enough?" queried the doctor. "Or go on?"

"Go on by all means! How about the women? Can they hold the office?"

"No. But fight most valorous for suffrage." The doctor trailed off in memory. "Oh, it be inspire. Be govern by Gogg and want say who Gogg."

"But they do not seek the office?"

"No. Vicarious satisfaction mayhap, in act of measure for select as Gogg. Be satisfy measure and choose Gogg. With suffrage, women rest."

"I think I understand that."

The doctor continued. "Be custom five month before expire of Gogg term and select of new Gogg, women also measure candidate free.

"Of course," warned the doctor, "other time be treason say incumbent not most big. Destroy stand Gogg have. Rule necessary preserve majesty of office."

"You sound more like a lawyer than a doctor. You know the laws, the decisions and the basis for decisions. On the other hand, you have said nothing about medicine or the symptoms of disease. How do you explain that? Do the doctors here study law?"

"Natural. How understand idiosyncrazy of men if not know law and rule of conduct? How advise course of treat in marry relation if not lawyer? Be rule, all doctor be lawyer. But all lawyer not be doctor."

Longfellow had a number of questions to ask but the doctor-lawyer stopped him. He held up his hand.

"Enough. Be enough. Let satisfy inner. Dinner wait. Do welcome to eat at table after recent experience."

As they walked to the dining room Longfellow mentally recapitulated.

What actually had happened? He had landed on this place called Goggle, been examined physically and rudely by the people, and saved from embarrassment by the doctor — all in the crash of his capsule. When he had come to his senses, one of the first things he had seen was a woman with exposed breasts or was that a phenomenon in his mind's eye? Such an explanation would reflect his hope rather than reality. The hours of loneliness in space could have created fantastic imaginings.

Ever since the world began, man, though he had had to cast an occasional look at the rest of the world to do it, had admired himself . . . whether he called it surveying, studying, looking things over, comparing, examining or inspecting. So Peter Longfellow flattered himself by looking at the world. He knew he must probe carefully. It having been his fate to be cast on this planet where there were other people, no matter what the hardships, he must suffer them through so he could report back. His world would be intensely interested in this place and these people. Not to study them at first hand would be a crime against civilization and a dereliction of his duty. He would try to be very scientific. He would look into each of the practices of these people so that his report would be complete and accurate. He would draw no lines. As a true scientist, he must not.

While thinking these thoughts, Longfellow collided with a chair. He bent over and examined it. "Your chairs are very fine," he observed. "What interesting wood!" With this observation he turned and watched for the expression on the doctor's face.

"Wood? We have not wood. Chair be stone. Volcano stone."

The answer told him nothing to guide him in the discovery of materials to help contact the world he had left behind, but if he kept alert Longfellow was sure he could extend and expand his discovery. Investigation, like a sister of cross-examination, required skepticism, cynicism and the asking of questions, all with great skill and diplomacy. Longfellow knew he had qualities to do the job, though he had not been trained along that line—because he knew he had them. But he must not offend his host, for with his friendship, Longfellow could gain support and help. He would remain open-eyed to all the possibilities, building friendships upon which to call when needed and at the same time do sufficient research for a report on the people and their state. It was an exciting prospect. His world would acclaim him as a discoverer.

The doctor's voice brought him back. "Sire, permit to present O Perceiver; and daughter Palpater."

Longfellow hadn't seen the women come in but quickly said, "How do you do?" His regard for the family grew as his eyes quickly surveyed the appearance of the ladies. He never noticed that the women only nodded in response to his "How do you do?"

They were a family picture. O Perceiver he guessed was thirty and in her prime while Palpater seemed about sixteen and was blessed with a full complement of Peter One blood; Peters of the highest order, both. The mother at the peak of her beauty or just turning the corner, added the intelligent maturity of her years to her face, giving strength and softness to match the hair on her ears. When she smiled the ears moved, waving those fringe hairs. Bullet hole eyes of clear blue were set deeper than those of the doctor but not so far apart. The hair on her head was thin and blonde—what he could see of it showing in wisps from the edges of the grey bandana turban she wore. The jaw was sharper than that of the doctor, avoiding the impression of toothlessness although when she moved her mouth her ears rotated forward and backward like compensating cam gears. Longfellow admired the shimmer of the cloth which offset so remarkably the soft flesh of her bosom, noting that in all things these people eschewed color. Everything was plain and colorless. The soft hair which grew from the ring area around the woman's nipple though strange was not offensive. It even offset the boldness of the bare breasts to make the display more correct. If her face was not what Longfellow had always admired in the past, at least the breasts were full and firm and Longfellow remarked to himself that motherhood and maturity had not destroyed the perfection of O Perceiver's lines. Below the waist she wore the familiar cuirass showing thighs muscular and legs set solid. The fuzzy hair on the legs which contradicted the principle of cover and uncover which the doctor had said was the plan for their clothing could easily be ignored.

Longfellow turned his study to Palpater. Similar in outline to her mother, she had a round, square jaw line and darker down on the upper lip due to her dark hair, with small, sensitive nostrils in a flat nose not so broad as her father's. A turban head cover wrapped around her neck matched a filmy white cloth which served as a frame around her two inverted cups. The hair of her nipple rings had been brushed back in a circle to make each teat look like a pink eye with surrounding lashes. Her loin cloth was tasselled, swaying with her movements as she sidled around a chair, and Longfellow could see she had no truck with the affectations of those who used the razor when they could not boast a natural culture. He ignored the hair on her limbs to prevent losing a full appreciation of her other bodily attractions.

Suddenly an inner perception reminded him that neither of the women had said anything though he distinctly recalled having said "How do you do?" to them. That was rather curious, though perhaps it had no meaning at all. The food was on the table, set with four places, and they were all waiting.

The doctor suggested, "Sit we and eat?"

"Why not?" Longfellow bowed to the women. Neither of them said anything.

The doctor carved substantial portions for each from a big roast. Longfellow studied the roast. It seemed to be one piece, with the appearance of the meat roasts which he was accustomed to. Blood or gravy oozed from its pores. There had never been any mention of animals, or what the basic food of the Gogglers was. The roast didn't appear to be vegetarian. There were other dishes on the table which were different, and they were served separately. That would be as he knew it, the extra dishes containing the vegetables. Most likely they had a special place where they raised their food. He could ask bluntly what the roast came from . . . but this might seem offensive. He would wait and when the time was propitious, he could learn about such things. Right now they were eating and he forgot his curiosity and his qualms and pitched in. Except for the sounds of cutting and chewing, there was silence. His curiosity about why the women didn't talk and how they sounded when they did talk piqued him. He fished in his mind for an interesting and striking question to ask. He looked to O Perceiver. "I'm afraid I'll eat you out of house and home after being lost so long."

She nodded and a fleeting smile appeared on her face. Or was it something he took for a smile? To his right, the doctor replied.

"Ah, worry not. We be flatter and honor thee here."

"Thank you."

A little miffed, Longfellow turned to Palpater to continue his stimulating conversation. "I trust my being here will not disturb nor upset your normal living."

He thought these challenging questions demanded an answer but Palpater only nodded and smiled. At least, he told himself, she had smiled openly. But the doctor answered for her also. "Be good disturb. Be delight have thee."

It was like being an unwelcome guest on a visit, where the hosts are too polite to tell you so. Longfellow, ill at ease, listened to the doctor and glanced questioningly at the women.

"Perhaps law in country be differ," the doctor continued. "Peter One say and we observe careful, women not permit speak immediate before or during meal. Nod when address. Very strict rule."

Longfellow relaxed at this sign of the devil's hand. It was not too difficult to adjust himself to the fact that neither of the women, at whom he only dared cast glances, could answer or talk to him.

"No," he admitted, "that law no longer exists where I come from. I know of no place where they still have such a law, with the exception of Goggle."

As though he would have a peep behind the scenes, he studied the faces of O Perceiver and Palpater. What could go on in their minds while they were being reminded that they could talk only at certain times and under certain conditions? Was it cruel? Was it unusual punishment?"

"This law," Longfellow tried to talk while his mouth was full, stopped, chewed his way to the end and then started again. "This law was passed on by your supreme court?"

"Sire," there was the faintest sign of indignation in the doctor's voice. "Court pass on every law. Law be for hundreds years and all agree about wise and necessity. Women have place but not talk while men enjoy fruit of life. Man not enjoy food if women talk!"

There was a note in the declamation which especially struck Longfellow. The doctor had used the word Man as referring to the species on Goggle, whereas in earlier talk they had been referred to by the doctor simply as Gogglers. Of course, now they were speaking of the present—the cultured and civilized present. A wry contortion from his mental picture of the law's operation gave slyness to his question.

"How far does the law against speech by women while men are enjoying the fruits of life go?"

"There Court and Peter One disagree. Law apply to every situate where man derive pleasure. Women be enjoin from interfere with such pleasure by chatter or make noise."

"In all situations?"

"All! Rule apply equal to what Peter One call pastime, but later Court rule it proper women quiet when men work; and not spoil appetite by say to distract, or by talk. But declare uncustomtutional insist women silence with men at night. 'How,' ask great Chief Judge Popoff the Ten, 'could man expect woman be quiet, and still get full pleasure? Most demand woman flatter constant, to satisfy ego.'"

"Popoff argue further, say, 'How be woman at best if normal, simple comment of wife be interdict?' In addition, Judge commentate in public commentary, 'One need realize actual of life. Women not can remain silent; most particular true with man these love. Could lovebird be silent during mate season without destroy self; be adverse to public interest.' To prove equity, for it require much courage and persuade to rule Peter One be wrong, Chief Judge Popoff the Ten, urge 'under particular circumstance which then ponder, silent be more great distract than speech.' Popoff rule be law since. Many Judge and commentator disagree, but law remain."

Through the relation of this history of sexual interdiction Longfellow cautiously glanced at the women. Far from feeling queasy they watched the doctor and listened intently.

Every now and then Longfellow glanced over to study the walls or the table or the food, and found the women within his perspective, particularly their elegant—he could hardly say it to

24

himself—breastplates. What a study! Either because he had been starved so long or because he wanted to finish quickly, he found himself gulping the final mouthsful of food.

After they had finished eating the men rose and started for the living room and the women followed. The room was a little on the pretentious side, with great cushioned divans and large down chairs, their softness being opposite to the severity of the chair he found in his room. Windows without panes let in a balmy breeze.

"Sire." Charmed by Palpater's soft and resonant voice, Longfellow saw the pupils of her eyes contract and he absorbedly watched the movements of her full lips and determined jaw line.

"How happen be there," she jestured in the general direction of outer space, "in small float?"

"Not a float—a space capsule. My booster went awry and I was lost in space."

The blank expressions on his hosts' faces told him they didn't know what he was talking about. "I'm an astronaut." Still no signs of recognition came. As he was first to get here since Peter One, how could they know about capsules and satellites and flying and planes. He'd have to start at the beginning. For only a second he wondered how Peter had arrived, then he brushed the question aside and talked about himself. "We have machines that rocket through the air."

His words brought excited questions. "Thee fly? Thee fly like bird?"

"That's right. We have such machines and I fly one for my country."

Palpater looked at him skeptically. "Thee fly here?" Again she jestured toward space.

It was easy to keep her interest, Longfellow decided . . . and desirable. "We fly into space and are in the process of exploration. When we get lost, for space is endless, we just float around."

"Be fooling," commented O Perceiver, her voice showing the same resonance as Palpater's, with the fibre a little rougher.

"No. Far from it." The women were now in the conversation, and Longfellow had reason to look at them. Always having prided

25

himself on his straightforwardness, he liked to look a man or woman in the eye when he had something to say to them.

"You see," he picked up the thread of what he was telling them, "we have been sending up space capsules for some years now and I am one of the astronauts."

"What be purpose of trip?" The doctor joined the questioners.

"I was on a job for my government."

"Be govern man? Be great help develop system for govern people, do hope. Thee know natural function body politic, and can guide as did Peter One. Help push into most great advance."

What could he say? Could he tell them that he was the kind of government man that could only fly in space . . . and then, only when he was catapulted there by a force others controlled? If he were to serve his people, he must, like all good government men, accept the assignment given him and do whatever was asked of him, even if it called for greater experience and strength than he had. He knew, like all good government men, that the people would never know the difference anyway.

His silence caused the medico-legal expert to repeat his question. "Will help?"

"Sure, be glad to."

"Job for govern?" Palpater inquired curiously. "Be secret?"

"Not any more. Time is very important and by now the next satellite has blasted off and the search is complete."

"Search?"

"Yes. I was out on a search." With no interruptions he continued. "Let me explain. We have been trying to contact Saturn in our solar system to see if there are human beings on it. We hoped to carry our system to them; to spread the rule of justice and law; to get along with them without fighting; to find a place where we could do good and have it appreciated."

"Amazing," the doctor said. "What civilize! Be indeed thing aspire to. What culture! We appreciate!"

Longfellow's head sagged and then jerked up as he caught himself falling asleep. The doctor noticed his condition. "Be very

tire and extreme inconsider of we to keep talk whe
rest."

The women got up and went out of the room arm in ⸲
was no good-night.

Longfellow didn't dispute the doctor's statement. It
silly to do so for he was clearly exhausted, and had been
day after he'd been shot into space. Expecting the doctor t
and say, "Goodnight" he found himself listening as the
said, "Now, ask favor. As did tell, thee be in most great d
by Goggler as progenitor of culture and civilize child. Ever
gler seek culture and assimmolate and improve breed. These
many inducement."

"It strikes me," said Longfellow, although he had been
pared to go upstairs and sleep for twenty-four hours, "it str
me that with one man . . . in this case myself . . . being the pro
ator both for the mother, the child and the grandchild, as Pe
One was, it would constitute an extremely high degree of inbree
ing. Doesn't that affect the quality of the people who are born⸳

"Of course, affect quality. More pure, more fine, result of hig
civilize."

"No, I don't mean that," said Longfellow. "Don't you find the
mind affected?"

"Mind? More high degree culture, more high civilize, more
fine mind."

"Well, as the mind improves," asked Longfellow, skirting the
subject carefully, "is there a greater percentage of breakdown?"

"Ah, this be not sure," said the doctor. "Be more nervous.
Natural sacrifice for more great, compensate of civilize. More
great civilize, more fine mind, more great percent get too fine."

"I see," Longfellow said. "I have wondered about that because
inbreeding, I believe, has the effect of weakening the mind. What
did you say about the people wanting to see me and give me
things?"

"Yes," said the doctor. "Be what I tell. Thee be great in demand. Goggler make offer gift, and as favor to we, before other
Goggler know, and thee too great in demand . . . before other on

Goggle be service, hope thee accommodate we. Here, while be here."

"What do you want me to do?"

"Be perfect simple. Assimmolation. Want O Perceiver have child with more great degree civilize, more pure skin, more fine feature, more delicate mind . . . all these. Wish for woman and for Palpater too."

Longfellow sat and looked at him. Amazed, nonplussed, he felt all the incredulities that go with a disbelief of what he had heard, and he questioned, "Doctor, this is a most unusual situation for me. You are asking me to join your wife and daughter in the most intimate of human relations. Don't you feel any jealousy at the thought?"

The doctor was surprised. "Jealous? Certain not. Why jealous? Woman not go because like better . . . woman and I and daughter . . . in fact, most people on Goggle be interest only in best offspring possible. Most fine. Most pure. Jealous be point at pleasure in sex. Jealous if wife enjoy and be only reason do. Jealous fear compare; fear give up treasure; clear-think tell levelhead reasonable person, assimmolate and pleasure be two different function. Goggler follow logic of situation and seek child, improve result be very much desire."

"It is considerably different with my people," broke in Longfellow. "There are a percentage who think the way you do, but most of them do not."

"Know mean. Some imagine pleasure from mix mate. When case, more perspicacious not mind if mate have pleasure with other. Important improve relation. Consider," said the doctor, reverting again to the thought that Longfellow would join in the union, "consider thee or Peter One . . . in eye of Goggler . . . be more great than Gogg. Now," he turned to Longfellow in a manner that indicated there was no possibility of disagreement; his tone was friendly and winning, "who complain about connect with most supreme in heaven . . . like heaven father."

"I can see your point," said Longfellow. "Tell me, as a matter of curiosity, did the Gogglers mix this way between themselves before Peter One came?"

28

"No," said the doctor thoughtfully, "be true come only increment of culture, but Peter One show sole way assimmolate and Peter One teach Goggler good, healthy, procreate system improve breed. To get back to what say, allow us first enjoy benefit? Improve culture and civilize and breed this family first? Not know what desire, but what have or power get, thee name I supply."

"But . . . it just isn't right." Longfellow objected, "A woman and her husband are one. To have such a relationship between a woman and a man not her husband violates all precepts of decency and propriety. The Bible, our religion, has taught us never to covet another man's wife. Adultery is a heinous offense; a felony in some countries and punishable by death in others."

The doctor sat back in his chair, and studied Longfellow for a short while. "Be say thee not like wife—or only cooperate with daughter?"

"Oh, no! I am saying nothing of the sort."

"Not willing even with daughter?"

"You are misconstruing my words. I think your wife—and your daughter—are lovely. They are desirable and even exciting."

Longfellow stopped to measure his words and weigh what he should say. His former thoughts about the doctor's wife and daughter waved to his subconscious in temptation.

"The idea does offer prospects of great pleasure. It's only that I think it would be dastardly for me to do this to you after all your kindness."

"To me?" The doctor was visibly shaken. "I speak of wife and daughter."

"I know that. It was only a figure of speech. I would be violating your rights—your family relationship."

"Perhaps I not understand. More willing if give money or gift now—in advance?"

"No. No." The issue seemed hopeless to Longfellow—whichever way he argued, the matter was being taken on a personal basis. Better go ahead, he thought, and at a more propitious time, make the doctor, and all the Gogglers see how horrible was the course they were treading. How unfortunate that Peter One had conceived such a plan for taking advantage of their simplicity.

Peter Longfellow had an idea he should be civil to the doctor and his family and if this was what they wanted, he would do it. But only this time would he serve their demands. It would be a sacrifice, but . . . in the circumstances, civil.

"Money and gifts do not enter into it," said Longfellow. "You have been very kind to me, and I will do this for you without any gift."

"That," replied the doctor, "be most generous Sire."

The last word made Longfellow wince as he stood up to go to bed. Thanking Longfellow profusely, the doctor walked upstairs with him to the door of his room and left. When he was gone, Longfellow went into his room, disrobed and began to put on the pajamas he found on his bed. Before he could finish there was a knock on the door. He hurried to button the pajama jacket before he responded.

He opened the door to O Perceiver. She had changed her clothes and the housecoat which covered her completely made her lines most interesting and intriguing. A seductive series of undulations filled out the drape. The embarrassment which he had felt about offending by a too-close look returned. Longfellow moistened his lips to talk although he had no idea what he would say . . . his feeling being more like that of backing off and running . . . now that this woman was so close.

O Perceiver apparently had no such qualms. Her attitude was intimate and friendly, even a little forward as she came toward him. His heart went beating at his stomach. The women he had known passed in burlesque review through his mind as he recalled their shyness in comparison with the behavior of O Perceiver. But not even a flicker of a smile rippled through his mind at the preposterous thought of shyness in a woman voluntarily in a room with him for the intended purpose prearranged by her husband. With his mind frozen, thinking was out of the question.

In order to pull himself together, he excused himself and went into the bathroom. No sooner was the door closed behind him than his mind relaxed. It was one thing to batter at a closed door, and quite another to have an open door beckon to him. When he had been out with women in the past, it was a game where he played the aggressor and the goal was not always realized. Now, the goal was seeking him. Only now did he understand how different was his training all through life.

Stepping out of the bathroom he found O Perceiver lying on the bed, her physical contours shaped up in enveloping curves, her housecoat covering everything and hiding nothing. Languidly she turned and tried by the magnetic enticement of her hands to draw him to her. When he failed to respond, she bent forward in his direction. "What be wrong?"

"Nothing. Nothing at all. I . . . I . . . I . . . ."

Without waiting for him to finish his sentence she patted the bed at a spot near her.

Longfellow moved toward her hesitantly, and sat on the bed. O Perceiver relaxed again, lying stretched out alongside him. Matter of factly, yet gently, and provocatively, her hand stroked him.

"O, my Gogg. Peter." Her words expressed amazement and descended in pitch to the most intimate of caresses. His pulse increased and his breathing became deeper.

"Ah, Peter." The slow, honeyed tone in her voice seemed to draw him to her into an enveloping trance. Drawn on by the tone and the sighing, he kissed her. Surprise and an air of mystery suffused her face. Her hand touched her mouth, and she commented with the voice of an enchantress, "Nice."

Again she drew him to her, held him off coquettishly, coaxed him to kiss her. "Gently, Peter. Gently, Peter. Love be paradox. Be violent and yet must it be gentle and sweet in most violent and tempest moment. Peter," her voice cooed and whispered, stirring his erotic impulses, "permit I touch lips to thee"?

It wasn't bad to be the quarry under the right circumstances, thought Longfellow. All the tensions, fears and dreams through which he had been carried during the weeks he'd been lost in space suddenly left him in a great flowing wave of release. Relaxation put him to sleep.

It must have been several hours later when he was awakened by Palpater, and he felt refreshed.

"Hello! Have you been here long? I'm sorry. Please ask your

mother to forgive my rudeness . . . and you too. Sleeping in your company is not very good manners."

To her smile she added, "I sit by feet and wait. Until ready . . . I sit wait."

Longfellow reminded himself that he had made a commitment to the doctor. He arose from the bed and drew Palpater to him by the hand. Walking around her, he looked her over carefully and then unhooked her breastplate and cuirass. As the clothes dropped on the floor she stood like September Morn, hiding what her clothes had previously left quite exposed. The posture caused him to give her a questioning look.

"Be bashful. After all," she argued, "never be undress before man."

"Well," replied Longfellow, "there isn't much difference between the costume you are wearing and the clothes you wore earlier."

"No differente? Clothe all off!"

"Yes. I see that, but the exposure isn't much greater. You know, I think that thing which you drape over your shoulders should be called a gown. Then lower caste women would find it difficult to imitate you. You would be above the crowd—unique."

Palpater was delighted. "Gown," she said with a proprietary air. The thought seemed to charm her and she looked dreamily into space. Her hands went to her shoulders where they held up an imaginary dress and she repeated the word, as much to herself as to Longfellow. Her embarrassment at being naked had passed.

"Palpater be first on Goggle thee reveal most new name for shoulder drape." Her pride swelled as she breathed deeply. "Palpater enjoy consider of new Peter for first benediction. Gown. Gown. Palpater set fashion." Down on her knees she went and threw her arms around him. "O, Sire!" Her voice was filled with disbelief.

Inspired by the great kindness bestowed on her, with a choke in her voice she repeated the words, "Oh, Sire." Her eyes stared before her, but Longfellow knew she was seeing the imagery of conquest over other women.

Getting up, the girl threw herself upon him and for a moment he almost fell over, but he held her off gently, quite touched. He spoke in soft, tender tones, just as though he had not heard the words from O Perceiver a short time back. "Gently, Palpater, Gently. Love is not as violent as . . . well, as its moments. A person can be wild with love of another and yet be gentle with them. Love is gentle and sweet in its wildest moments. Come," he urged, "kiss me. Gently or harshly or firmly, as you feel it." He was so charmed with this creature that he did not feel the hair when he fondled her breasts. Violently their bodies joined, and he interpreted her cries of pain as those of pleasure. His senses drew inward the force with which they exploded.

Longfellow awoke next morning to find no Palpater, but the bed and the room were the same as the night before, and the dream was real; he was still on Goggle.

He dressed for breakfast. The women were not present. Both tired and rested, Longfellow attacked with hungry pleasure the food put on the table. Drinking a hot beverage that tasted like coffee, stomach full, he told the doctor,

"I had a wonderful night's rest."

"Did?" There was as much wonder in the doctor's voice as there was question. "Women?"

Longfellow was embarrassed to talk about them. But then, perhaps talking of what had happened would disturb the doctor and make him discontinue the adulterous farce. "Were the last ingredients necessary to complete satisfaction and relaxation of the body and nerves."

The doctor weighed his thoughts.

"No doubt there be some Peters able meet exigency of situate. But, in fact, most Goggler not. If try supply need be tire and exhaust for days. Thee feel better. All in order?"

"Oh? Oh, yes." Longfellow caught on. "Yes, very good. Exciting, sophisticated down to the finest points. Your daughter, naturally, is new but your wife was most avid, ardent, and yes, even eloquent. There is little she does not employ with great skill and persuasion. You are to be congratulated on her abilities, my friend." Longfellow dwelt on the last word, as though he were recreating the impression and embossing it on the doctor's mind.

As they walked into the living room he heard the voices and noises of a considerable crowd. Through the window he could see a line of Gogglers leading from the door of the house and stretching out for some distance.

"The crowd? What are they waiting for? Are they patients?"

"Patient?" The doctor smiled with an odd twist of his face. He wiped the grin off his face before he added, "Well, these like discuss ailment but ambition of assimmolate come first. These be wait see Thee. These hear of New Peter, and from early, line form for see Peter. These ask, offer gift and if thee grant wish, make prepare."

The doctor's mechanical smile was smug. The Gogglers were waiting with a prayer for Longfellow's grant while he had had all the benefits. He had the most assimmolated and most cultured and most civilized family on Goggle; and if he was nice to Longfellow, he might have him living in his house, almost as if he were a member of the family.

The doctor's gratification swept away all thought of the moment. Hooking his right arm under Longfellow's left, he led him away from the window. There was a twinkle in his right eye.

"Visit of thee reach ear of Gogg and he send emissary, ask see. As lawyer, do suggest we go. What say?"

"Whatever you say. But what about the crowd?" suggested Longfellow. "Shouldn't I see them, after they have waited so long?"

"Right way in democrazy?"

"Positively. In a democracy everybody is equal, even if they can't vote, but if they can vote all the more so. Each one, big or little, caste or no caste, is the same. One vote for each voter."

"One vote for each? Who vote for these who not vote?"

"Those who do vote."

"Be unable to follow." The doctor's face was puzzled. It had already become obvious to Longfellow that the doctor's mental reflexes were slower than his own. The way he screwed up his face when he was trying to understand, would be droll if it were not so grotesque. In this regard, the doctor seemed to sense his own incapacity. He said, "Capacity of Goggler be limit. Unless be show

34

by most simple word, in most simple progress, be not able understand."

"Well, Sir. Those who can, take care of those who cannot. In that way each one has the equality to which he is entitled."

"Mean all be count and these that vote, vote extra for these that not vote?"

"No. No." Peter pondered prudently. "Those who have more, need less equality. Those who have less, need more equality. The very young need more equality. And so on up and down the scales of equality. And that leads to justice."

"But what be equality? Do animal, like early Goggler, get same as Goggler today, like man? Be young equal old or old equal young? Do stupid equal smart? Do equal mean equal treat? Or mean it equality?"

"Equality means that all are alike and are entitled to equal treatment in dignity, respect and the right to express their opinions and vote for their choice—if they qualify to vote."

"But different between early Goggler and late Goggler be most great."

"No. I don't think so. The early Goggler was governed by force. The strongest asserted their control and each was given according to the power he could exert. At present, equality is determined intellectually. Those who control, by vote, or power, or financial influence, only vote for what is to the best interests of all. Never for their own selfish interests."

"But what when interest of vote against interest of not vote? What when vote be only interest of some?"

"Always the vote in a true democracy is for the best interests of all. If only a portion are better served by the vote, then there is no vote at all."

"And some suffer because not vote?"

"Perhaps. But unless a majority approve, in a true democracy, none are served."

"Excuse slow wit." The uncomprehending look on the doctor's face reminded Longfellow of children trying to add before they knew their tables, and this plus the doctor's general physiognomy and his occasional tendency to jump up and down when he was pleased, gave Longfellow the unpleasant feeling that he was holding conversation with an ape. He promptly rejected this notion when the doctor in an intelligently frank way apologized. "Be still not clear."

"Let's take it from the meaning of the words equal and equality. Equal means to make equal or level; or to represent as an equal, or to liken, or compare. It also means to become equal; or to produce something equal to. More rarely, it means to cope with on equal terms. Equality is the condition of being equal in amount, worth, in intensity, in dignity, privilege, or power; it is being fair, impartial; it is equity."

The doctor in his quaintly befuddled way looked at Longfellow. It was becoming clear to Longfellow that no amount of explanation of the principles of equality would make the matter clear to the doctor, and Longfellow struggled with the problem. Even if he could not make it clear, he couldn't say that he couldn't make it clear. He couldn't escape the dilemma of discussion. The doctor rescued him.

"Perhaps equality mean all thing be relative and most high intelligent be necessary understand principle and most high intelligent be equal—and this be equality."

"That," said Longfellow, giving up in despair, "is it exactly."

The doctor was delighted. "See. Be much thee teach." Then, pointing in the direction of where the Gogglers stood, the doctor asked, "See all Goggler, or choose?"

"How can I choose when I know nobody? They're all strangers to me."

"Be true. But Goggler have same wish, bring wife or daughter, or both so Peter decide assimmolate for improve race; and bring gift to help thee choose."

Longfellow returned to the window. The very idea outraged all his beliefs, and he determined that he must stop this practice and teach these people the right way of life. The sooner it was done, diplomatically of course, the better the chances of success. He should see them one at a time and explain his views, and make them see and follow the right course. "Doctor, could you let these people know that I will consider them in the order in which they apply? They should submit themselves in line."

"And wife, and daughter?"

"Why, yes."

The doctor left and told the crowd to return the next day with their wives and daughters for whom they sought service, and to form a line. As the word spread, the Gogglers broke up and left. Longfellow watched through the window, wondering whether he had in any way hurt the opinion these people had of democracy. He was about to question the doctor further when on second consideration he decided that what he had to say could wait until he saw the Gogg.

With yesterday's dazed feeling gone, he developed a little excitement. The visit to the Gogg was sure to be exhilirating.

As he was about to address the doctor, it struck him forcefully that he had never heard and did not know his name. Somehow this did not seem improper; it did not seem that he was missing something. He could call him doctor and it sounded right. But as a lawyer, the man would have to have a name and one by which he could be addressed. As they started out of the house, he said, "By the way, counselor, what is your name? I've never heard it, you know."

"That right." The doctor thought a moment as though he had to make up a name, then said, "Most Goggler call doctor, even when use as lawyer. For Peter that be improper. Name be Perceiver. Dr. Perceiver."

"Perceiver," repeated Longfellow.

Of course. O Perceiver was the wife or woman of Perceiver.

They had been walking a short time when they arrived at a block of stone, more square and formal than the doctor's. Its simple severe lines leaned away from the center on one side and away and toward the center on the opposite, like a left-handed drunk overloaded on the right. Longfellow studied the structure for several seconds. Either the Genie who poured the stone was leaning or his tools were awry or perhaps there had been no form when the volcano erupted and poured lava as though it

37

were making pancakes, layer on layer. He could even see where a fork had been stuck, leaving broken lines.

The entrance to the Gogg's place was nothing more than a hole in the white stone. They were met by a young Goggler who, like almost all the Gogglers he had seen, carried himself in a sagging erectness, his arms hung loosely and long and his knees bent slightly in a posture that suggested he might leap any second. He was dressed to expose his less hairy areas. In the instant while Longfellow looked at him, he performed the same somersault Bulbo had, only he flipped backward, reversing Bulbo's direction. Immediately after his gesture of obeisance, the young Goggler ushered them into a tall room, with the usual nondescript lack of color and imagination. The walls leaned like a child's box recently abused by someone sitting on it. Behind a desk near the entrance sat a broad-faced Goggler of middle age. His head was bald; his ears stood at attention. Obviously he had been assimmolated to the top of his head. His tiny eyes, unadorned by lashes, had a brightness that made them attractive. Under the eyes were crow's feet. The man was broad of shoulder and as he rose to greet them Longfellow noticed that his arms hung down to a few inches from the floor. His torso was much longer than his legs; and his pot-belly indicated a well-fed life. There was a show of servility in his bow as he approached them, but no flip-flop.

"Welcome Sire." His long arms swung forward and back.

"Your Goggship." Longfellow acknowledged the welcome formally.

The Gogg invited them to sit in chairs that had the same volcanic appearance and structure as those in Perceiver's home. After they were seated, Longfellow was kept busy answering the Gogg's questions about where he had come from, and about his complex and progressive civilization.

Suddenly Longfellow asked a question. "How was it first decided that ten years should be the period of Goggship?"

The Gogg looked at him as though the question was not clear, then, assuming he knew where Longfellow obtained the information, and the meaning of the question, he answered.

"Lawyer not explain thing in evolution. First Gogg select for life . . . ."

Longfellow interrupted. "But from where comes the choice of ten years as the exact period of shrinkage of the penis?"

The Gogg held up his hand to indicate he was coming to that, and Longfellow waited.

"Much time back, Gogg not popular. On advise of Peter . . . " the doctor interrupted him. "Gogg," the Gogg stopped without looking at the doctor, waiting to hear what he would say, and the doctor explained his interruption. "This too be Peter and we need decide call Peter, father of Goggle, Peter One."

The Gogg's grin of understanding spread his mouth from ear to ear as he repeated, "Be Peter Two," pointing at Longfellow.

Perceiver nodded aggressively, his head going forward and his tail backward as he canted while standing still. The Gogg imitated him; both chuckled at the joke.

Longfellow broke in, "The choice of ten years? How come?"

The Gogg hurriedly replied, "Peter One say Gogg, who has most big when select, be shrink in only ten year, five winter, five summer."

Sardonically, he turned to Longfellow during the last part of this recital, watching the lawyer out of the corner of his eye.

Before Longfellow could make any comment or give his opinion on this profound logic, the Gogg rose abruptly. "Sorry, but busyness attend. Have dinner with us?"

The invitation was directed to Longfellow who glanced at the doctor. The response came from the doctor.

"Certain Goggship. Bring for dinner."

Bowing, Perceiver turned and left, with Longfellow trailing. Once outside, they hurried along avoiding people.

"What did the Gogg mean, ten years—five winters and five summers?" Longfellow inquired of his companion.

"Mean? Mean summer year and winter year, five summer, five winter—ten year."

It wasn't too difficult to accept the fact that the Goggler year was measured by the winter and summer seasons, but Peter

39

Longfellow couldn't imagine why Peter One should make the years so short. Puzzling over that he asked,

"I assume Peter One set the yearly periods."

"Did," replied Perceiver. "Measure of time begin with Peter One. Year, month, day, fix by he."

Casually, Longfellow asked, "How old are you?"

"Be thirty. Soon be old and die."

"Thirty? Old and die?" The answer was confusing. How could Perceiver be thirty and expect to die from old age? At what age? Thirty of summers and winters? Or thirty divided by two, one year for summer and one for winter? The impossible calendar challenged him. And did that mean the Gogglers lived to twice the number of years he would live and yet the same period of time? The enigma had to be cleared up. Peter Longfellow pursued the question, "Do you mean thirty winters and thirty summers? Or do you mean thirty, half of each?"

"Thirty summer, thirty winter be sixty. Goggler not live after forty. If assimmolate, Goggler life might be extend like Peter immortal hundred-fifty."

"How," Longfellow questioned most seriously, "does the life span affect other phases of your life? By the way," the thought came to him in surprise, "how old is O Perceiver?"

"Be thirty-one."

Keeping Palpater in mind, he pursued, "thirty-one of your years?"

"Certain."

"And Palpater?"

"Fifteen."

"Fifteen?" It seemed impossible to conceive. "Fifteen summers and winters?"

"Not." Perceiver was himself amused and then puzzled. "O Perceiver only fifteen summer, sixteen winter. How Palpater be same?"

The whole program of life and death was mathematical, mused Peter Longfellow.

"First," he asked, "how long does a mother carry her child from conception to birth?"

"Five month."

For a fleeting second Peter Longfellow thought of asking about the method of reproduction but having participated in that himself he decided he knew. The next step to him was, "At what age can a woman conceive?"

"Begin fifteen, like Palpater."

My God Peter thought, that means the Gogglers conceive at seven and a half of my years—and that Palpater was only seven and one half. He visualized the woman who shared his bed and shifted his fantasy to O Perceiver. She was thirty-one of Goggle years, which was fifteen and a half of his years and had a daughter like Palpater who was ready to have children.

"If O Perceiver is thirty-one, at what age is she too old for children? At what age does life end?"

Perceiver turned a sad face to him. "Forty old. Thirty-five end time for child. Most die forty, quick fade some thirty, for sure fade thirty-five."

At this point they were on Perceiver's street. After they had entered the house Longfellow suggested that he would like to go on up to his room and rest. The doctor encouraged the idea; and then a sudden thought came to him.

"Would read words of First Peter?"

"Words?" Longfellow's puzzlement showed on his face and in his speech. It had been his impression that no one on Goggle could read or write. "What do you mean?"

"Peter One write and leave with family. Have here." Walking over to a special alcove, Perceiver drew out a sliding shelf on which sat a volume; he took it in his hands. It was a bulky tome and the pages could be seen to be thick like parchment. Handing the volume to Longfellow he said, "If wish, take."

Longfellow took the book and thanked him, and carrying it in his hands walked upstairs to his room. The book was not so heavy as its size suggested, and when Longfellow glanced at the pages he found they were written in an awkward and untrained hand. The sheets had been bound into the volume with stitches. Casually he sat down in a chair and began to read.

Just when sea seem calm, I feel raft which I make of mast scooped up by wave, with self on top, and cast through air like harpoon.

Part II
PETER JENKINS

MY NAME be Peter Jenkins. I be to sea ten year since I be lad of fifteen and did ship as second mate from port of Liverpool on sailing ship 'Mary Cross,' bount for Indies. We be three months at sea when ship run into typhoon. For few hours we fly on power of wind at so many knots in one hour I believe it not. None of crew could do aught but hold near support, and then great sudden we fall in hole in sea, water come on us like dropped with meanness and we fall apart at seam like box which fall from height. I know not what happen to other members of crew. I never see these again. I find self tossed about, hanging to fifteen feet of mast. Storm still blow and waves toss so hard mast submit and bend over in half. Very fortunate for I last fibre of wood hold two part together so mast fold like jack-knife. Some of rigging be still hang to one end and I realize great advantage to keep two piece together, so I wrap rigg about two pieces and tie. I know not how long I be toss about . . . whether it be six hour or six day. The storm so heavy there be no day and there be no night.

Just when sea seem calm, I feel raft which I make of mast scooped up by wave with self on top and cast through air like harpoon. There be hot air and mast and rigging rise like kite. For long uncounted time we fly. Then come flash of land, heavy blow, and blackness. When conscious return I be in strange place on floor of leaves. These people which be around did frighten me at first by appearance, for these look like shaggy beast of whom I had seen stuffed figure in museum. With speech gruff and gutteral, walk like ape, and face feature so close to animal I fear I be captive of tribe of monster. Be strange gutteral speech to me, and yet, as sailing man travel through all Island of Indies and up and down Africa Coast and on inland water of South, I did make out meaning, when speech be help by gesture.

It did take not too many week for I to learn the speech and what mean and so with much talk and more gesture with hand, and dance with feet I did learn this be island in sky which these brutes call "Goggle" and that head of tribe name be "Gogg." I had not injury but only shock, and did suffer exhaust and exposure. Quick be remedy by fine treatment receive. Manner and manners of these, for I did treat these like people, be deferential and respectful to me and in short I decide to use experience and cunning to be King on island and have all. Before I make plan I did meet all of these, to see what these be like, to see how these conduct selves, and learn what I want. I learn how become leader of island. What rule? I discover from he, that biggest be leader and be select by Goggler, when he also be strongest and beat all on island.

I fix measure of time in year to be based on season. Day of year when sun show self for shortest time be new year, and day of year when sun show self for longest time be also new year. This way I make note odd year be winter and spring, and even year be summer and fall.

Gogg be huge brute but also very fair and listen to other and in especial to I. I find self able to convince he what right and what wrong in all situation and soon he respect me as be of great wisedome.

To take more great advantage of position with simple people, I study situation. Chance of return to country from which I come be remote and better for I to make best of things. From moment of land, Goggler admire smooth skin of mine, and it seem miracle

44

to these I have not hair in most part, for these be hairy all over. Even female be full of hair.

Gutteral speech and funny gesture be easy to master and I quick learn to communicate. Always these ask about pale and clear skin and whether other people be like I. I explain this be natural condition in my home and it did come about by custom where lead man of country be King and father of all child. Though these did have no female that be attractive, they be female and I spend long time at sea and have no woman for long time, and after while these female look to me better each day. I realize too that with such weapon and many promise it be not difficult to get whatever I wish and control Goggle. As I do write this log forty year after arrive, from log notes made as did go along, I not yet know whether Goggle be island in ocean, spot in sky, or place in hell. Preacher I have hear when I be young, say such activity as I encourage and follow only suggest hell; other I did hear at same time say it be heaven.

Whichever case, for I not care what be right for other so long as I think it be right for self, I begin advise that free from hair be due to Kingly custom of masche, about which I did hear. This as I did understand back home be right of Lord to first night with any female in domain. I tell Goggler also, King have sex with any female as kindness to female and family for by proper breed female give birth to offspring that have not hair. I not know whether this be but I be sure when time come if offspring have hair, I blame Goggler for cheat and suggest it take several generation of exclusive custom.

Custom of proper breed I call assimmolation, and I tell Goggler and these believe because very gullible and because these want to believe. First female I lay with be female of Gogg for he be most anxious to have first assimmolate child. I be surprised at great acceptance, for soon all on Goggle demand service for female—mother or daughter. This surprise follow by more surprise when I learn that Goggler female carry offspring only five month; and that these live half of time I live. Twenty of their year be only ten of mine; at twenty these people be middle age. At age of forty years, which be twenty of mine, these be quite old

45

and die. First child I father, after ten regular year be middle age and I be twenty-five when I land so then I still be only thirty-five.

As King, I be entitle to wealth and position, and Gogglers bring gift and establish I in regal fashion. So anxious be Goggler to receive service and so willing be I to accommodate that within six month make with child all fertile female in Goggle.

Not all offspring born free of hair. First sign of improve be slight. But there be slow improve, and this did make Goggler joyful and believe. When offspring be fifteen their year, which be only seven and half mine, these mature and ready for childbirth. Improve come only by repeat breed with King, which be self, and when offspring be ready for childbear, mother and male consort bring these for further assimmolate. This increase demand be both pleasure and burden. For be require I take care of mother I first inculcate as well as daughter; and beside I begin find offspring more stimulate than mother. I assure Goggler that male offspring perform task for older one, also instruct that at thirty-five of their year, female have not right to be further assimmolate. Between thirty-five and twenty of their year these could breed with male of Kingly union which did reach fifteen of their year. Goggler become complete interrelate.

In thirty-five year of mine, which be seventy theirs, I be sixty and there be five new generation in direct line. But since mother carry child only five month and breed be repeat soon as possible, there be generation or new line every one year their calendar and I see there be seventy generation though separation of generation be only by one year. All Goggler on island when I did land pass away long ago. To later generation Goggler I be immortal, and prowess be legend for in generation that did come and go, word of mouth about Peter, father of country, pass along and multiply in retell.

Many generation have effect on Goggler, which I do call people, for these be child of mine. Many female lose hair and some develope two full breast. Yet some have one breast and some none. In matter of hair, result be irregular. Amount of hair determine caste, for Goggler with much I treat as low caste and insist these must receive breed service from offspring, not self. Strange

46

it seem but after many year I develop dislike for hair, though at begin it not matter to me how dark and hairy these be or even if these have breast or not.

I also teach women many innovation and trick and idea, all to excite and stimulate I, and these trick become custom on Goggle. Design and name of clothes, kind of law system, kind of govern these have. Always I did retain Royal Kingship.

After number of generation pass and after I set up Chancery Court and teach Goggler of system, and while engage in study law to make more change, I one day sit with Gogg of that time when messenger call. As messenger enter he did flip-flop to floor in recognize of superior and King. When head come up, and hairy face look at Gogg, I see had he purpose and message.

"Gogg," he say grave and serious, "clerk of Court send with extreme danger and anxious news. Case file by Hoora, ask to control govern—right vote, right rule."

I did eye messenger without understand . . . it be much twice made talk. What happen must be personal decision by I.

"Who be Hoora?" I ask, for tho all on Goggle be offspring, I remember not every child and name of such. "And where fit he and why do these consider action serious?"

"Hoora bring case?" Gogg wife faint upon hear news.

I help Gogg move female to chair and Gogg run for servant. While I wait and try to fan she, I think this be serious. Gogg bring two Goggle female to help Gogg female.

"Now," I ask, "what be about?"

Gogg took turn at chair very sad—just as would I if King sent me for trial before hanging Judge during bloody Assize. I wait answer, he relate problem.

"Sire, as do know, number Goggler," he shake hair free of face to clear thought, "percent number Goggler, few year back show insane on increase. Count show be one per cent more Goggler insane than other year back; and rate on increase; increase be so much great, force gather like move of time."

"Thee tell us Sire," he remind, "matter not some be in asylum or out. All be Goggler with same background." I remember so tell Gogg for it matter not to I if some be in or out, or if some

47

vote or not. I be Sire of all and let thing go as go. Some be one caste and some be other, but I be above all and take or use what I wish. Perhaps, I think, I did concentrate overmuch on one point. Perhaps, I think, I should attend govern session but it seem that not interfere be best.

Gogg talk more. "Last year, half population in asylum. Alarm sound, but Sire, thee think it not important and we not able to stop grow of crazy Goggler. During year we fight against tide, but more go beyond wall. Last week, spite fight and struggle, medic figure show one more Goggler in asylum, than outside asylum. We hold breath in fear, for Hoora, leader of in-group, aspire to Goggship when I be select. Preach and build insane group to follow he."

"But," the Gogg say to I when I ask, "thee insist and say how else true govern be run? All have right to be hear."

"So," say I. "He be hear. If Hoora seek aid of Court be no danger of violent. Be believe in pacific."

Gogg tell I of danger. "Hoora seek Logg (This be name I give House of Lords, which be top Court) say insane group caste be most number of Goggler. So before small number he argue now be bigger. When these be majority, must be consider normal and have right enclose other who establish asylum principle."

"Half population be in full control of govern can keep Hooraer and all these where be, and prevent take over and stop threat to position and safety?" I retort.

"Sire!" said Gogg. "Thee order us be nation where majority rule be absolute. Thy order be absolute and we abide in principle and give control, whatever result, though Goggle be torn and destroy. Never we surrender principle or swerve from magnificent standard."

This Gogg say very noisy, as though to vast audience, before fall back to dejection. Very soul of contradiction.

He believe so firm in system he see Goggle destroy before retreat from firm belief . . . . At same time, have no faith, for gloomy forecast be destruction if idea of democrazy be sustain. Sorry for he, I decide remain aloof from fight between offspring.

Gogg jump like Goggler of work. "Sire," he plead, "stay with

48

woman of Isham whilst I call Goggle politician. It relieve mind great to know wife be in thy hand."

"Woman of Isham?" I ask playful.

"Yes," he say, "My woman."

"Speak of she with no name?"

He look at I most curious. "Name, of course, she have. She be Woman of Isham."

I remember old country custom when marriage make woman know by husband name. Call in playful sense to Gogg, "Thee say Woman of Isham? It be obvious she be woman, why should say Woman of Isham? It enough say of Isham, and it mean same thing. Be thy woman speak of."

Quick he get idea and accept so easy I push little more.

"Gogg," I say as he about to rush off, "Of Isham be awkward. Need not be so. We had way in old country of say 'O Isham' when mean thy woman, or 'O Boy' when mean Boy's. It be just right."

He nod to me. "Yes, Sire. It simple system. Tomorrow," he say, turn away, "I make law for all Goggle."

I slap he on back, eye in back of head gleam, "of a certainty I buoy up O Isham to make forget what face she."

Gogg hurry out and I find O. Much be learned from she, who be Lady before these marry. Though seem strange that self who father all Goggler not know each and every offspring and all about and what go on, it be not so strange if remember how many. I see mother only short time, and I bother not with male offspring. Strange to ask about system I did make, or ask about judicial system I establish. Or about politic system I create. Easy see why misunderterpret.

I learn Goggler Perceiver be head doctor at asylum. O Isham talk of Judge, refer to one not on bench; talk of Senator Syes; and Professor; and Grave Represent. She know opposite leader; name, record, and character of most inmate of asylum.

Interest in O Isham rise new. Flat first impression be change and stimulate by much she know. I make firm friendship and get better view of Goggle so I write great log.

It be few days before Logg hear Hoora case, and I and Isham attend session. We walk to Court in grave silence. Stone door swing back easy and inside be most high and lofty room. Air be cool and rare. I think any minute bald bird of prey dart for I. Place most austere and I sit in seat set for self. Goggler swarm through room like bee through hive, in spite of empty corridor we so recent did pass. Curtain up front rise quick and expose sudden, like row of doll in human size, thirteen Judge behind bench that run zig-zag from one side of room to other. This be part of design I order but forget. Judge be in full regalia. Chief Judge Popoff, descendant offspring from family of early time, look like head doll in Punch and Judy show. Wig of bald skin show suspicion of curl from edge and wig glisten with sweat and have more life than Popoff.

All other Judge sit with face to wall behind. Each of twelve other wear mask down to shoulder, and false face appear on side of audience. Back of head, with mask face cover, be so design to fit section cutout top of chair. I turn to counselor neighbor.

"Be not interesting arrangement?"

"Yes Sire," say he. I forget it be I who establish custom. "Old member, who be appoint in early regime, be familiar with old rule and tradition of Court, and sit look ahead. New judge, appoint by present Gogg, not vote on law he pass. Look back these judge must, to rule which exist before now, for instruction and guide in law. Though look back at old law, cannot vote on new, as thus would permit current Gogg to change law for immediate use."

"And Popoff?" I like to ask and have Goggler tell rule or history, tho it be I who made, and he, many generation off, not know this.

"Oh Popoff be appoint by now Gogg's Gogg, and not possible to have desire to aid now Gogg."

"Why masquerade? Why false face and cutout chair?" I manage to ask without show in face I be joke.

"New Judge sit face back to keep steady remember of old rule and tradition of Court."

"Go on, go on." I break in.

Lawyer be surprised at outbreak but take time to resume.

"To keep dignity of Court, and show respect to Goggler, mask

Curtain up front rise quick and expose sudden·like row of
doll in human size·thirteen Judge behind bench that run
zig-zag from one side of room to other·

worn by new Judge have face on back so Court show proper front and at same time look back to feel full weight of tradition."

"And cutout chair?"

"Back of chair be cut out so face which appear, mask and skull, be not obscure. As result, new Judge support own head."

Clerk, old and slow-voice Goggler, hold up hand and announce, "Court in session."

This be difference I develop on Goggle from legal rule in old country. In old country arguer or orator or barrister, whichever these be call, sit wait for appoint time and when case ready for argue, Judges file in like prisoner let out of cage. On Goggle Judges be already seat and when Clerk drone out title of case, barrister be let in court room in single file, each special for field, good or bad.

First barrister speak for petition group be call Pease-Pease. He be broad of beam, sloven and loud and aggressive, like Captain of "Mary Cross." On Goggle all with big rear, dirty and loud, be call Pease-Pease as I advise should be. After, walk in Judge Beadle. Then come barrister Upright and Downright. Thirteen Judges most solemn 'til Chief Judge wave hand indicate first party argue. Pease-Pease stand.

"Thine Honor." Voice be loud and strong, impress like good monger of public ware. He repeat greeting of respect. "Thine Honor. For many year, we follow principle majority Goggler rule. 'Til now majority be outside asylum. We accept rule. Inside asylum, Goggler be not permit vote albeit in sound govern, these should vote. Now come we to Great Divide. Majority of all be in asylum. Client maintain three things. First, group have right to vote. Second, being majority group, have right to govern. Third, being majority, what say be right must be right, for in govern voice of most great number be proper.

"Whoever put these in asylum, when be in most bad mood, refer to these as have poor mind and as be more low than nothing. This be not true. Scientific person, particular medical men who examine statistic on subject, know all in asylum have antecedent. It be after grow and develop of culture that mind become finer. Stage at which mind become so fine person be in limbo where govern group call insane, be select at random. Why at that point and not at later point a little more fine, to say insane? Or that point and not a little more soon, to say insane? Either point make difference of ten per cent of Goggler who should be in or ten per cent who should be out. Why not one or other? Point of select be arbitrary. Up to arbitrary line, Goggler be clever, brilliant . . . in fact, genius. Push beyond and automatic be insane. No longer consider clever, or brilliant, or genius. No, for that matter he have not mental status . . . and this be theory of govern group . . . he be less than most stupid and most low class person outside asylum.

"It be our position that these in asylum, who do now constitute majority, far from insane, be most clever on Goggle. These have most fine mind. These be most assimmolate. More advance in culture; these leave other far behind. This petition, made in accord with democrazic principle, ask Court decide, not that these in asylum be majority and rule, but that any majority rule. Fundamental law. It work out more great number govern. If this Court believe democrazy, it rule majority establish norm and majority take over."

Pease-Pease sit down mid silence.

Dr. Perceiver be next to I.

"Why," I demand, tongue in cheek, after jostle Dr. Perceiver, "should Goggler like such be in asylum? What wrong with he?"

"He?" Lawyer-doctor manage weak smile. "Pease-Pease be just lawyer for insane."

"What?" Great feeling flow over I at delicious joke. "Why should" . . . I ask Dr. Perceiver question he should ask self . . . "Why these appear and argue so forceful and sound that they be now in minority and shud be class as different from norm? Why argue thing which change own life . . . affect living and position . . . danger family?"

"These have not choice." Perceiver show great understanding. "These be lawyer, honor member of honor profession. Every Goggler sane or insane be entitle to full and fair hearing. If Goggler have not lawyer it not be full and fair hearing. What chance do ordinary Goggler have if be no lawyer to act for he . . . explain distortion . . . twist away misunterpret of all he say, even when

53

cause be most just? No, Sire, we of honorable profession always fight for Goggler . . . it be duty . . . it be bread no matter how it affect we."

Court look now to whiskered Goggler who take part. Tall and straight he slow come to feet. Dr. Perceiver answer look by two word that sound like Very Upright. Such name be similar but different than I did long time back use and since did always hear but I accept as same order of different as other thing I did see. Barrister Upright speak slow but make word clear. I hear each word as if Captain bellow order.

"This petition must deny for many reason. Consider! Petition state insane form majority and should govern and full manage. These stand normal; we stand subnorm; et seq and per se that mean we be crazy. If so, this Court be deconstitute. If Court be crazy, how thee can reason? If cannot reason, how rule thee on such petition?"

He stop for second to look at Judge, first end one and then end other. Then he talk more.

"Next point of argue be: "To govern must know what do. Insane mean not know what do." Barrister Upright beat breast in anguish, wave arm and shout. "Can Goggler destroy all Gogglers build up? Can Goggler, in name of justice do unjustice to Goggler family?

"This petition be insult to all and what all stand for, and should unequivocal be deny."

When barrister finish and sit, entire line of barrister rise and in good military form march out. Court follow.

Next day back in Courtroom with Gogg I wait for decision. Judge come in first, and then advocate. Pease-Pease lead—Judge Beadle next, follow immediate by barrister Upright and Downright.

Goggler silent like wear sea fog in English Channel. Even whisper be silent 'til, at correct minute, Chief Judge Popoff rattle stick and talk.

"Matter petition Hoora for declare insane normal and right to govern, Court unable arrive at decide. Face with history Court

54

not agree. Each member vote and give opine . . . . But no decide because no majority of one opine."

Popoff falter minute, voice weak. "Hoora speak in real for whole group though he be one. At first idea, suggest by petition be revolting—ridiklous. We who committ fellow Goggler as insane, think of govern as belong only to us. We praise govern—claim govern—and practice govern. Confront with propose to give govern to group we say outlaw, sense of importance be outrage. Idea be very radical. Indeed it be very radical. But it be reason. We consider purpose and method of govern. That place rule in majority of Goggler . . . most great number. Since radical constitute more great number of Goggler on Goggle, I believe these be entitle govern. First, we permit they vote. If insane present more voter than caste in power, these be establish right of Majority . . . right govern and set what be norm for all Goggler. Before vote I say fellow Judge Batt who not vote, and refuse decide, be outrage. To vote one way or other be duty . . . patriotic duty. By fail vote, Batt prove he traitor. I vote for."

All in Courtroom stir, but none more than Gogg and Dr. Perceiver who be on each side me. Judge give opine one at time, and next be senior after Popoff. Judge Titlock clear throat. Younger than Popoff, he turn rheumy eye, and voice so crack as to be difficult to understand. Hand did shake.

"Disagree with learn brother. Let me, as said Judge Popoff, consider purpose and method of govern. All be state in phrase 'for most great good of most great number.' Grant petition give most great power to most great number. But do it most great good for most great number? Answer clear . . . No. To do good insane must show know of what be good. Before such time these must show abile to proceed with vote or govern process. Petition seek break tradition. This be radical and I give such name to these. Judge Popoff say petitioner be capable. Insane not see own deficient. If these not see that, then mind be twist; these not sound choose for Gogg; and if not make sound choose for Gogg, cannot carry basic customtution rule of govern and fail before begin. I reject. Join brother Popoff in condemn brother Batt, and charge fail vote and refuse vote be treason."

55

Eye of all in Courtroom turn to Judge Batt who, though in center of all eye, turn not face from wall.

Next in senior opine be Judge Piddle, two place remove from Popoff. Voice strong and clear and opine short.

"Theory of democrazy not require he who vote know for what he vote or how govern. Be no law such; no case so hold. Whether so-call radical have reason or abile be not material. These have majority—and majority rule. Petition should be grant. I join condemn of Batt. Avoid of duty and oblige of duty be treason and coward."

Abrupt as Piddle finish, next Judge, Pinchbutt begin. Vigor, youth resound in voice. "Hold Goggler must know what he do before he do. Equal for vote and govern. If no concept of obligation; not know duty, not understand what do; and not can vote, not can be governor or govern. My opine preclude insane. With not know, be not democrazy. Petition reject; condemn fail of Batt to answer duty."

Air of Court be tense with vote tie two two. Goggler in audience whisper. Excite make crowd breath loud. Judge feel tension in air and these proceed faster; each give opine as one before finish.

Judge Muddle next. "Must have norm civil life and abile for vote. If not norm how vote norm thing? How tell what norm— what not norm? Present argue be quibble. If insane agree with we, these be sane. If these not agree . . . not conform to rule we do make for conduct . . . these be insane. Gainst petition. Gainst Batt."

Judge Totington give voice. "Assume these must make petition and present to Court which exist at time. Court operate on sane standard which petition ask reverse entire. Be so different and outside what Court recognize, Court cannot recognize these or approve insane. Deny. Condemn Judge Batt, also condemn colleague who not agree with self. Condemn barrister who degrade profession by present outrage petition."

With last word Totington turn and slam hand on Bench so violent wig go awry, reveal hair cut in tuft.

Smile form in corner Gogg mouth, as vote turn.

56

Tired voice of Judge Morehead belie young look. "Same reason advance by Judge Muddle; to-wit and wherefore; these all be normal and abile for vote; if not normal, these not vote. Petition should be grant. What majority do be normal and establish normal life and ability. For more, if these not normal not vote, and normal change with more great number, who now vote be deny right to vote. And Judge Batt be condemn."

Judge Grossteste take turn to decide. Mark on wig not initial, but mark identify for brother in law. I learn he only one which be lawyer and doctor and work some each.

"I," say he, "have live in institute where Goggler dream . . . where live in separate world. I. too, live in place of own. I too spread wing to fly on wind of imagine. World where body be . . . be fill by body. Mind live life more excite than real world. Assume," he continue, and intone word like liturgy sung in church, "by gain majority these call radical gain right vote and choose; and assume again, as friend Totington, these present petition Court which exist at time of demand, this court. Though Court operate on now sane standard, such standard change with change, and practice be moulded to time of apply, not time of practice. Say I, we arrive at conclusion in Court which serve most Goggler and what be rule at time, be sane rule at time, and Court operate sane. Vote petition be grant."

Serious of situation with vote four each clear. Five judge more to vote keep Court tense, and Goggler sweat and mop.

Judge Brakass say, "This Court have not jurisdiction. Gogg make law in Goggle—Court interpret law. Court not to legislate. Go to Gogg for decide. Gogg pass law. Vote no."

"Agree with Brakass," say Judge Dunghill. "Be case for legislate, not interpretate. While so agree, feel need new help of King." Judge then look at I. "Advise and guide and instruct how law fit awkward situate. Deny."

Next offer of opine and wisedome be Judge Skandl. "I," say judge behind huge pair glass, which have not glass, for Goggle have not such material, "think as Brakass. Because for law, not interpretate. Gogg pass law. Issue writ Gogg pass law give radical right vote and govern. If Court not agree, I vote for. Result not direct but result consciente dictate."

Order next of senior, Judge Batt, to vote, but turn hand palm up which be signal not vote, and Judge Nosemore speak.

"Judge Dunghill express essence. Be matter great wisdom, brain wisedome need omnipotent somebody. Differ between animal and other species, animal have abile think. Not just think . . . but think in imagine level. When we not allow mental agile go to level of imaginate, we thus punish Gogglers for idea strange to us.

"Suppose other animal, not see or dream like Gogglers, say we be wild . . . fantast, that we be so to such. How know we whether creature of dream, fantasy, we claim insane, not unusual . . . be real on different mental level? Mayhap we hinder free develop. Mayhap animal have no abile think past get food — and condemn who abile think beyond. Mayhap mental evolve be only begin sign of new think. Mayhap forefather think on such level. Mayhap radical belief Goggler die and come back in body of different level and communicate be impossible. I vote grant petition and case refer for advise and help. Democrazy come first and if by Gogg it work, Gogg agency implore for help."

After he sit back record be tally; six be for petition and six against, with Judge Batt refuse vote. So be no decide. Judge Batt apologize. "Feel, like other twelve brother, I know not what or how vote. Not like other, I not abile vote on such condition. Let other call traitor — coward — or else. Mayhap these be right assume be good patriot whichever vote and I be traitor vote not one way or other. Important be truth, not shadow by not know. No vote cast I 'til arrive at decision."

Judge sit quiet behind Bench like becalm ship, as barrister line rise and move off stage. Court member then rise, face left and march.

Roar of Goggler as talk all at one time break. "What mean?" ask Gogg of Upright and did answer self. "Trouble think me. We need do some and I believe know what. As thing stand, thing stand."

Gogg bend over to barrister, mystery like. "Need work out

58

plan. Give radical right these demand and at same time protect we 'til we do overcome these . . . in democrazy way, of course. Remain all for cooperation."

"What be do?" ask Upright.

"This night we meet and make all clear. Radical win petition . . . insane get right they ask . . . and all be right in little while."

Gogg look at I significant but say no more.

Gogg home be den of conspire that night as Upright and Downright arrive. Mystery fill air. "What Gogg plan?" I ask. Upright eye light for second and light eye improve flat face. But no answer.

At about time these settle in chair Judge Batt appear. Be he traitor for refuse vote? Be here by trick or promise? Fire eye belie weakness and suggest strength and determination.

Gogg tell plan. Quick voice give impression he fear not permit finish. "This be plan. By rule of democrazy, what most large number want must be done. It be very essence of true justice. Radical be majority . . . we give what these demand."

Gogg eye comb face, see if any require special persuade. Gogg continue.

"Same time law give customtution guarantee individual not molest. Each entitle life and liberty. We not can guarantee conduct of radical after take control and must place restrict on these 'til sure." Quick voice stop as he glance over each rapid. "All agree?"

"That," Judge Batt say with care "depend on plan. All law compromise and each need yield. What propose?"

All watch with attent as Gogg tell outline.

"Simple. Radical claim govern because these have most large number of Goggler. These have proof if allow vote. Select of Gogg be long before insane take over. By that time these show intent; and that time, when radical not yet in power, we be free and protected. Decide," Gogg turn to Judge Batt, "need have reserve that radical prove to Court in year these be able of govern—of run election and vote and select Gogg."

"While wait time, do reactionary, as one of brethern term

59

sane Goggler, vote? Will these govern?" Batt bend forward and sharp dark eye focus on Gogg.

"Present govern continue 'til new govern take over, else be chaos. Let radical hold convention, elect leader, decide method, and decide do these permit conservative vote, in election year from now."

Judge Batt meditate. Not easy won, nor fool. "How soon for convention?"

"Sooner quicker." Gogg speak and plan interest Batt. Other sit back.

"If be too soon, these not able run convention right, these not know what be about, and fail prove these run govern." It be challenge of good intent.

"Set time. More long away, more better for we. But not fair to radical put off very far. These work as group for year, while in asylum. These have leader and long delay bad as no wait."

Thinkful, Batt wait. Gogg convince he sincere and Batt measure plan. Finally he say, "All right. I do. Not because thee urge . . . and not because democrazy dictate . . . but because think I otherwise insane revolt and cause blood. I vote yes on morrow, on condition radical prove by conduct in elect period, capabile self govern. These must hold convention in five month and show able govern and decide if conservative be allow to vote and how set up govern."

Seat throw Batt forward, or so seem, as he bound out anxious to get from conspiracy. Other walk back to den arm under arm. I follow.

"Now," Gogg take lead. "Outline be only half. Other half need us cooperate." Turn to me.

"Thee see," explain Gogg, smile over face show please with self. He allow potbelly protrude so he pat it comfortable. "Take five month for convention . . . period for select. In that time, if we go about diligent, with conservative help and cooperate, be born enough new Goggler to conservative to swing majority in populate count."

Trick clear. Last day of year new petition be file in Logg and whole process go back. Radical then back to asylum.

"Be not thing overlook? Conduct not conservative. Be very radical." I say curios.

"True. But imperative survive or continue control."

"Every one know it be radical conduct and say we be just copy these." Downright say with same idea as I.

"No special right to conduct, and Logg never stop us from adopt and follow plan. Mayhap Judge help." Gogg answer.

"What if radical do same and whelmover us by number?" Downright demand.

Gogg say "Not announce or let know we do. Urge conservative quick and great increase." Look at I. "Thee, Sire, be sure change to high culture and if thee work with conservative, caste rise like hound from burr. We list all conservative and if radical make same demand, thee take all, in order of ask and conservative be first on list."

"Suppose radical understand and go on own?"

"It be chance. We start long before these realize. Relax law so female have young—mate or no. Young join too." Gogg say with spirit, "Even month start, give advantage. In democrazy, these come first be serve first. We prepare list . . . only those out of asylum . . . answer reasonable and correct."

"Be justice?" I ask.

"Why not?"

"Be not fair, equal treat if who enjoy benefit of manage and control refuse chance to other at same power," say I.

"Follow rule exact. Majority rule. We do work at get back majority."

"Thee refuse give same power thee have?"

"No, Sire. When these control, these have same power."

I taunt, "And thee be sure these not control by fix result."

Gogg and Upright resist most fierce. "True democrazy," argue barrister, "be by will of majority. If majority change, will change. Fact we urge Judge Batt vote for petition be proof of integrity. Fact we wait year be only prevent radical from drastic act between time."

I shrug. Think to self what differ? These caste or other. Who know?

Gogg say, "Need help all young. Conscience objector be punish—or compel. How old thee, Upright?"

Upright show worry. "Not old . . . not old. Age be as feel and act . . . not year that pass over."

I continue think this entire plan be for own benefit and purpose. It be right for radical, asylum caste, know what afoot. If I tell true opinion these think I tell to save self from service. For good . . . at least to give radical fair chance . . . I lie.

Take self to asylum to see Dr. Perceiver. He be surprised pleasant and take me through asylum.

"Doctor," I say most cordial, "be not more safe, for continue majority of radical in asylum, to have more child? If do little, while Goggler outside most active, lose majority to conservative."

Perceiver take idea most fervent and then hold meet with Hoora, Senator Syes, the Professor, and Judge Eagle.

Dr. Perceiver tell other, I advise great increase in propagate and culture. Remind, I father all Goggle; all assimmolate and caste improve . . . and through me, hair on body disappear, and child, and child child, become pretty.

Necessary assimmolation, I give these more attent than conservative, and guide these rapid and true in propagate faith. Assure I cultivate radical female so gain most great number, and Hoora, the Professor, Senator Syes and Judge Eagle, be govern Goggle.

Myself believe I fool conservative by increase radical, while conservative think these enjoy more great assimmolation. Lye I on both side. Most great fun . . . most delight of pleasure . . . most amuse of game . . . most hard work in life . . . be in next five month. Doll of past, mother, daughter . . . fat, skinny, smooth, rough . . . these all I serve. Women enjoy measure, and when stop fun, do more if reason clever. So pass harrow and hilarity period, and convention time come around.

Respectful noise at door tell self guide arrive for take to Radical convention. King and Sire need all honor. I study these as stand in living room . . . . Fellow, Well, Why, Ho-ho and Victoria be name of mate of these female. All be outstand female which

62

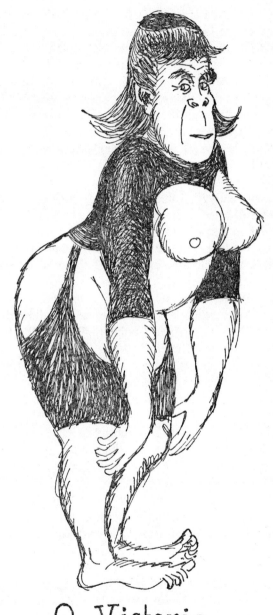

O Victoria

receive special attention from self. Sixth female enormous size, I not remember see before.

O Well introduce she. "Sire, this be Pulpa."

Pulpa bow, fall on knee, for too huge to bend, and kiss my finger. I be fascinate. Great bulk still show outline be female. While Pulpa kneel to me, still kiss finger, thought about escort to convention run through mind. Six female? How proceed? In history book, King go by coach. Be proper ask? No, top King take for grant all do should be do? Female recognize pensive mood and wait 'til I look at these.

"Well," inquire I, "we go?"

"Majesty ready?" Pulpa, look up from kneel position while kiss finger, roll over on back.

Behold I in surprise O Well and O Why and other. Without hesitate, O Well take one leg of mine and O Why other. I put arm around neck of each for support and these raise, and sit I on Pulpa like on camel.

"What! What!" "What! What!" I demand.

"Sire," O Victoria speak, "as Sire we not allow thee walk to convention. This be carriage," point to Pulpa, "thy throne. This be symbol of seat top Goggle."

"But, but . . . female Pulpa," I sputter, "She not suffer?"

"Suffer, Sire? Suffer? It be most great honor."

Pulpa confirm by shy grin. I accept. Astride she, I feel pillow all over.

Female bring canvas web which by quick manipulate be slide under cushion steed, one leg up, then other, then arm. Be done like diaper slide under baby. I hold Pulpa so as not to slide off. Pole set in each of four corner of canvas and whole, Pulpa and self on top, be raise. Slow and rhythmical these march.

Radical in procession path bow and salaam. We curve and twist through gauntlet of adoring crowd, and we march within line made by many Goggler. I ride like Indian Potentate in howdah on elephant . . . Goggle elephant. I bounce self to enjoy cushion, and think to self I never get rider cramp so.

Crowd shout extra huzza when place of convention be reach. Litter bearer enter hall, march to head table where food be and

We curve and twist through gauntlet of adoring crowd, and we march within line made by many Goggler. I ride like Indian Potentate in howdah on white elephant.

set Pulpa, with me astride, down. O Well stand right, O Why left. I move to climb down but O Well take hand and restrain.

"Sire, be seat. Please to relax."

All around wall, which curl like circumbendibus and create niche and dark corner, radical Goggler of once high estate filter to place. Many politic leader go to place at table.

First mouth of food I eat be signal for other and these attack food voraciously. For hour these eat without sound of speech—of mastication plenty. At finish, these did wait for sign from self and I decide test power.

"I tire. I think I sleep for hour." Most convenient I stay where I be. Loud so be hear over hall I speak. "I sleep for hour."

O Well and O Why raise I off Pulpa and while these hold I O Ho-ho stretch my legs. Then arm. First one, then other.

Pulpa roll out from under and O Victoria lay down. I be set gentle on O Victoria so back and bottom not defile by touch chair or floor. I relax while O Ho-ho knead, twist body, loosen neck muscle and turn head gently in many direction. Soft and supple finger rub face and head and soon I drowse. Pulpa return and I restore to position in such way I lay back and sleep. Doze as hear politician begin speech. It be honor for me, but I fade to sleep. Let talk, I think . . . and these did.

Sleep bring dream. Home after visitor find log book of Goggle. Give lecture of discover and experience, but none believe. Then dream change. Prominent person, famous for acid comment —woman with tongue which drip vitriol — publicly acclaim I. True or no, she say, log be great work of art . . . master exhibit of imagine. Temper of people change. Book be popular. These who did sneer at book of Goggle when not popular, be now friend. Seek brilliant writer who catch public imagine. These find me, no matter where I hide, and offer attention, home and friend. Be fun and yet not fun. I do shudder and wake to find O Why look in face apprehensive.

"What wrong, Sire?"

Blink eye to orient self. Quiet O Why concern by patt cheek. I raise self and look around. Right to make speech complete circle

66

of table and Hoora be orate. Voice reach climax and finish. "And now," I hear, "I offer toast to King Peter."

All stand and raise glass.

All empty glass. . . . Goggler march in file and when all move I be raise on litter and parade go round like serpent.

While I be carry through convention hall and out door to come in again on other side I turn in mind govern business? When Mary Cross sail, be talk of new democrazy and idea law make justice. As philosopher, for this I be call by two or three maid I visit in differ port where I spend time, I think of this.

To be philosopher be like lawyer and yet be not like lawyer, for philosopher not have experience and training. Lawyer pass detour and byway, which be at least six. Which mean be six differ way to see and get round fact. Lawyer avoid misstep where philosopher fall. Lawyer go direct to point in straight line round circle and side twist. Philosopher not know what talk when talk straight. If I lawyer, I be lawyer-philosopher, ideal character. Shake head in agree with what think and decide own profound idea need be writt down.

Lean over to use left mound of Pulpa as rest. Immediate, I need shift, for this be too low. Find right. In simple practice way, find support for general opine that right be more high. People say and what people say be true base. As philosopher I at once see proof of value and truth of precedent.

Finish write profound wisedome I realize what I think Pulpa right, be really my right and Pulpa left. While it true people say right be more high, this prove people wrong and one be not wise accept precedent blind. What people think not always measure to science test. I give test for size, weight, depth and firmness of right and left mound. Rising interest of I in problem be interrupt by O Fellow who call to I.

On new approach to hall we meet group female, most young. These set up cheer, many seek to touch I so these could say did have hand on great Peter. Costume of these be differ. It take no judge to tell these did tear and cut piece out of dress to look same as mature and married female of asylum caste. As committee of

67

six female meet these, these bow and each one at time, kiss finger mine. Ceremony finish, these then march.

Fat ball under self be set down in special place arrange for great Peter. I remain on Pulpa, which be throne, soft and yielding, yet self-inflate so no lump form to dig into side of I. Five female of committee stand by wait to service I. These work to make as much comfort as possible. Natural for mind to contrast this service and what I receive from conservative female. Compare what I see of sane female and extra service and honor these show to I. Thus be convince I right in help these. Be variation on variation, but I did have no doubt. Important part of work done . . . and well done, I be told by many.

From balcony where I sit, I see all. Place lay out in section, and hold 1000 Goggler. Plan have one represent for each five. With five thousand total for radical, one thousand be right. Much credit due radical, for committee make perfect arrange. In group, Goggler filter in hall, and though some look like female, only male be permit stay on floor and vote. Seat be by section group, and identify by small picture which appear over each sect . . . I give name to each. White . . . Red . . . Blue . . . Black . . . Green . . . Yellow . . . Brown.

Delegate stir about, some talk, some whisper, some laugh, some shout. Hoora, giant man, hair comb back and hold in place by ring of brass, walk to stand, reach under coat, bring out gavel and begin pound for order.

"Who be Chairman?" I ask young female who stand by I.

"Hoora. Be great Hoora."

Tone of female did please and I ask, "What be thy name?"

"My name?" Hand of female go round in circle and square as if she press invisible thing to shape. Chin flutter, she throw self to ground and weep. Between sob and sniffle, I hear repeat over and over, "Peter ask who I! Peter ask who I"!

I feel hand touch person and female next say, "She be Cuddle, O Well offspring."

Commotion in hall reclaim my attention. Hoora pound for order. By ruse he plan be Chair. Always Hoora be leader of Goggler 'til conservative reactionary, in majority, become jealous, and call he maniac and put he in padd cell. Now free, Hoora lead and soon leader on Goggle. First must be temporary Chair, for in good meet and in convention must be temporary Chair. Sudden voice from Green sect scream.

"Who make thee Chair? I be Chair! I have most money!" Goggler sing and parade round hall. "Lunatic from Jingo Paw, what be more"!

Green sect where Goggler stand slow take up song and join parade. Other Goggler shout, "Second nomination!" Candidate voice rise high on gay note, and group of follower hit high pitch. Demonstration delegate from other section, succeed to make group of Green join, sing same song with melancholy tone. Lunatic from Jingo Paw go off pitch to falsetto and stop. As Goggler wait for follower to sing and march again, Green group trickle back to seat. Immediate whole sect from Red desert.

Alone Jingoist take up song, sing each line in different voice so sound like differ Goggler. But rally fail. No more join Jingoist, who shout to Hoora, "Who make thee Chair? I have most money!"

Hoora bang gavel. While convention be of new majority and be abhor connect with old majority, he go by parliament rule which I did make. Hoora bang gavel and shout, "Out order!"

"And me?" Demand little fellow in Black sect, with drawn body and squeaky voice. He wear hair part in two place to make face look full and give impress that two head be better than one.

"What about me? I travel all over?" Little fellow add quick. "And up and down beside? Be not I acclaim hero and get medal?" He feel chest with both hands and, not find decorate, begin search on hand and knee. He trip number of Goggler and knock over chair and be pile up.

Hoora demand, "Be second?"

While chaos be straighten out candidate forget he candidate. From front of hall, in mid White sect, come dignify and correct voice.

"Great grandfather be son of revolution."

Revolutionary statement receive with concern by all delegate.

69

These look around at one another, uneasy to be see in presence of Goggler, and many turn to other with finger on lip.

Speaker stroke hair from face. When he stop, hair fall in circle on head. Speaker think not proper to demand right so speaker repeat, "Great grandfather be son of revolution."

Gentle rock as Pulpa inhale and exhale make I nod, but sudden quick bounce and jounce wake I wide. Pulpa be blow and gasp for air like whale. In sleep, hear say "Great grandfather be son of revolution," make she become excite. Movement throw I back to other in balcony. Recollect I, make Pulpa quiet and sheepy.

"Be all right," I assure with gentle pat, cover lapse.

Speaker announce, "I second own nomination."

Proceeding again claim attention. While delegate hunch self so not be see in revolution Goggler company, deep voice boom from end of hall below Blue. All eye turn in direction. Barrelchest radical Goggler, tall as broad, stand on chair look over shoulder Goggler in front. Beard stubble and flat two hole nose hide other feature of face, and little pig eye gleam from bristle. Voice be culture.

"Ah, gentle Goggler! I fire asylum. I Goggler of great deed and prominente."

Shout of "Speech! Speech"! arise thru hall. Hoora be brought from trance by shout and he bang gavel. Glad to make speech.

"Goggler, delegate, represent, and, ah, everyone here. Be democrazy and we go by Parliament rule." Sweep hand at hall, he declare, "All out order."

From part of Blue sect delegate rise, voice shrill over convention hall.

"I be Gogg. I kill bigg robber. I be most fame killer on Goggle. I kill bigg robber. I be Gogg."

Dispute come from neighbor. "Oh, no; oh, no. I be champion boxe and wrestle. I be champ. I be Gogg."

"And me? . . . and me?" Other neighbor same sect challenge. "I order kill all these outside asylum. These be no good. These be no good to we. I say these be kill and I be Gogg."

Last speaker disappear as sudden as appear, with help by surround hand.

"Poo," Hoora say. "I stir riot for two term. I run for Gogg ten year back, I urge radical rise and fight. Riot I say. Demand right. Kill some conservative and these listen. Rise I say, rise!"

He puff cheek, draw up shoulder and stand on toe so height be exaggerate. "Some year back, great alarm sound because half Goggler be in asylum," he wink broad, "And too many be crazy." Face break in broad grin. " 'Crazy' be what these call we interesting and unusual Goggler!" Delegates roar approval.

"Some year back when radical had fifty per cent of Goggler, who demand be allow vote? Who say vote for me? Who want govern?" Delegates look one at other but not answer. Hoora hair point in all direction while chest and shoulder puff again, and he swing side to side to prove he swing weight if necessary. Sudden dart at podium, thrust head forward and chin out as if take delegate by storn, then say, "As Chairman . . . ."

Voice in front of hall in White sect interrupt and yell, "I be Gogg!"

"Thee yell? Yell I louder. Come here and we see," shout Hoora.

Hoora competitor start walk to podium. Heavy and shapeless leg come out of torso so far from each other and straight down like pipe out of pot-belly stove. Head and face clean-shave look like large smooth stone. Neck lost in chest. With mouth open, huge competitor shout practice yell while he walk to stand swaying side-to-side.

"Now," Hoora say as Clubby reach stand, "let hear small yell."

Clubby yell small.

Hoora breathe deep and give most lusty shout. At finish, he stretch arm to group in hall, and these set up clamor.

"Hooray for Hoora! He win! Hooray!"

These begin parade round hall. Clubby shout he not have fair trial, but Red sect join parade and yell in unison with Hoora group, and Clubby drown out.

March go round in circle, every one carry sign with sect picture and here and there be sign with Hoora face. Most laugh and smile, each shout to Goggler different, some different word.

From balcony come shout.

"Hoora for female!"

Delegate begin to sing same. "Hoora for female!"

March continue many minute while see move of shadow from sun. Some delegate march and some not march and none give attention to other. Color of garment and shade of hair be many.

When noise die down, all parade back to seat and Clubby shout again.

"Want fair trial." Voice set up vibration over entire hall.

Hoora ask crowd, "Get he chance?"

Hoora follower shout, "Sure!" Red sect take up word, repeat, "Sure! Sure!"

"Who win?"

Hoora follower shout, "Hoora! Hooray for Hoora!"

Hoora wave Clubby to side and address convention. "Now I be select for Gogg, we do work."

From not far off I did hear very proper fellow call to Hoora. "Hooraaah." Sweet voice, he have hair comb from center head out, and be cut in fringe like petal of daisy. That and other reason these call he Daisy. When he stand before crowd and say nothing, crowd hoot and Daisy sit. Turn to neighbor, same time comb hair with hand so petal lay even round and I overhear he say, "Dear dear. Be so difficult to be personal to strange Goggler."

Neighbor reply, "Really?"

"Oh, yes. Talk to thee be differ. Thee see, it be like this . . . ."

Interrupt by neighbor. "I be stranger as all these."

Daisy bridle. "Well! Thee not understand."

"Not misunderterpret. I love listen."

Daisy unfold and explain. Alway fancy self as thinker, and though talk and talk, idea be boil down to idea. Distinction former norm Goggler make, always seem ridiculous. What be done be impulse within nature self. Yet norm Goggler set self as judge and consider action not action.

"If certify, do no wrong; if not certify, all be bad. That be what former norm Goggler say. If feel go with body, destroy feel or be wrong.

"Feel make like beast these say. Be confuse. These Goggler walk like lion and act like crow."

While Daisy talk, orator on platform begin with crowd and I turn attention.

"Therefore, Gogglese (this be few time I hear this word) and Goggler, I challenge Hoora right to be Chair, or to be Gogg. I, great Cadence, Goggler who set soul on fire, demand why Hoora claim right. Look at distinguish gather. Throttle-Bottle," he point, "author of many murder that shake world. And Gainboro, there," wild-eye shine from face to which Cadence point, "who advocate mass murder and stir Goggler to riot. And there be Plopp, most great ball player ever live. And there . . . but what use?" Out went hand in despair. "I forever name Goggler more in deserve be Chair than thief Hoora."

Several Hoora follower pull Cadence feet from under he, and general melee follow.

"Mr. Chair!"

Sound of words please Hoora and face spread in smile. Bow to White sect, from which Senator Syes address he, and announce, "Chair recognize Goggler with two hat!"

From front seat Syes rise. On head there be two hat, one black and one white. Black hat be on head and white hat be on black hat. I know significante of hat. When Senator in agree with what go on, black hat be on head and white over other. When Senator be in disagree, white hat be on head and black over other. When Senator not on one side or other of argue, hat be off. When Senator be agree with both side of argue, two hat sit on head next each, free for ready move to shift hat in middle of argue.

Be senator philosophie that all life be not consistent. Inconsistent not always consistent. At time life be consistent and at other time life be inconsistent. But inconsistent be hallmark of life and especial of Goggler.

Fame and experience and official title make he to know need to address Hoora with most respect. Deep Senator Syes bow to chair and after to body of Goggler in convention.

73

"Mr. Chair and fellow Goggler. Have now before we grave problem of minority; group call conservative. Decide, be influence future. Question be: be former majority insane because different from we? Question lead to next question. If be insane," he open arm in spread gesture to take in all Goggler in convention hall, "what do we with former majority? Incarcerate these ... change place with these ... put in asylum while we live in house? Let these vote?"

Many voice shout from other part of White sect. "Let we these vote? Put we these in asylum?" Voice interrupt from Blue section. "Point of order, Mr. Chair."

Hoora say, "No order be recognize without it be in fashion order. With thee not first make bow, Chair not listen. What be right, be right. All Judge know this; lawyer know; and justice (he lay left hand on chest) and sense justice, and do justice, be not listen, if not hear right word before listen."

Voice from Blue speak most respectful. "Thee have Honor. Thee be right. Most humble we beg for listen, advise and what be left of right."

Hoora reply, "Chair hear point order."

A thin and wizened little Goggler from Blue sect now rise. "Mr. Chair, fellow delegate. Decide of Court only allow we choose leader and decide if reactionary be permit vote. We not permitt to commit these as these committ we."

Hoora ponder question. Sudden solution appear in manner and he raise two hand to deliver great ruling.

"Goggler. In well regulate convention there need be platform. What Senator with two hat propose be not decide of commit other now, but what do after vote time ... be only part party platform. Party must tell voter what be future platform when run Goggle. Point of order be disallow." Hold hand to Senator with two hat, "Proceed, proceed."

Senator with two hat bow. "I accept amendment. Commit we these after vote period of select be over, and permit we these vote in period select?"

The crowd sat silent and Senator with two hat continued. "We have expert. Let be hear word on matter. Professor!"

74

Turn to old Goggler who sitt near. "Professor do know all about insane. He be with we for forty year."

Professor, mild and learned, nod.

"Professor," ask Senator Syes, "Can not we eleminate question of differ between reactionary and self, since these always insist be different? We determine only whether call these reactionary insane and whether insane Goggler be allow vote, and whether we change place with these at end of vote period."

The Professor nod sage like, and stroke face. After decent interval, he deliver opinion.

"On sanity question what majority think be normal. Therefore and whereas these who think and act different from me be not normal. Since minority, conservative reactionary, have by much record prove we not sane because of differ; since we be new majority and sane be what most great number of Goggler do, I say be no room for discuss. Act of other do decide question."

Hoora pound gavel on speaker stand vicious, and long after all be quiet, continue pound. Enjoy authority and leader and when he enjoy enough, he hold up hand, palm out. See hand out, Hoora sudden scream.

"No! No! I not suspend great gather without full discuss and detail. Want each be hear and each want be hear, though we do know decision. I decide when stop and final. This be democrazy and we go by Parliament rule!"

"Mr. Chair!"

Delegate from Red sect interrupt. Hoora voice change from deep tone to soprano.

"You speak Mr. Delegate?"

To convention Hoora order. "Quiet! Quiet!"

Red sect shout. "Quiet! Quiet!" and keep repeat 'til Hoora bang gavel.

"Mr. Chair." Delegate clear throat while fix tie and push shirt tail in trouser. "This body," he pause and in grand manner survey convention, "this great body of Goggler," he stopp again for emphasis and lose thought. Out come tail of shirt and he peer intent at tail before continue. "This great body of Goggler be meet to

75

decide what sane. This mean we not know. After we decide it be rule. Before we not know. Who say dement? Professor?"

Professor bow deep. "Peter not set rule for conduct and think which separate. Goggler do such . . . ."

"Mr. Hoora, allow not such talk!" Hoora turn to man in black with pinch and solemn face who sit in balcony.

"Reverend Grones."

Hoora insist on being call Chair. Mr. Hoora not enough; he like better be called Chair. But wait for Reverend without argue.

"Chair recognize Goggler from Up."

"Goggler! No one say Goggler establish two different Goggler —one Goggler and other.

"Be not everyone feel noble influence Peter stir within? Why . . . these put we in asylum because spirit of good come from Peter. These feel influence, and deny exist of Being that make these so or make feel that way. Be not evident of irrational? Not proof these be mad?"

Delegates cheer and shout so Reverend, solemn with duty, have to wait. Delegate in Blue sect, tall burly Goggler of hairy antecedent, try throw chair on which he sitt at Goggler much feet away. Burly upset twenty neighbor. With fury and frustrate take violent act against each near. Flail with fist and climb over shoulder and head to get Goggler he dislike. Hundred usher quiet Blue Sect and Burly and when subdue, Burly weep.

"Whole world gainst. He start and all help he. Thee help he. Be worse than conservative."

Usher whisper in ear and Burly break into smile.

"Thee promise?"

Usher nod and Burly shout, "Quiet! Delay convention."

So excite I lean fore and slip on Pulpa lap. Huge body contort at sudden move. Committee quick raise and lower self in seat. Pulpa say, "Sire!"

Quiet restore, Reverend Grone start again dull tone voice, head raise and eye fix.

Goggler hoot from Purple sect. Goggler whistle to keep he from speak, and whistle, stamp and slap—break over hall. Grone voice again pitch high like fanatic.

76

"See Peter! Speak with Peter! He show world proof! These not look."

Neighbor scramble to look and all in hall look to I and each find self crowd from place by other, climb over head and shoulder and body. New furor over, delegate listen again and Reverend unheed of dissent, continue.

"Supress long message from Peter. I be Him!"

Monotonous voice become screech and eye become more fix. Air of speaker be Fire and Brimstone.

Purple sect send series of catcall and hoot. One delegate throw hat to Reverend and Red sect erupt with more hat and food—all direct at Reverend. He not see and not hear! Reverend somber pace out hall, eye transfix. As walk, raise hand high, fist close in threat over head of delegate.

After moment pause Hoora turn to Professor. "Professor. Continue."

"Wait! Object! Disagree!" From extreme right, Blue sect baldhead Goggler stand. Fierce manner match Hawk-hook nose. Most unusual look.

Pulpa say to self "Judge Eagle. Without I see, I know voice."

I look down to Pulpa and nod.

"Great lawyer judge," add Pulpa.

"Chair hear from Judge Eagle. What be object?"

"Last speaker make not proper interpret of rule. What be insane in religion? I tell thee. When Goggler deny exist of Peter or commit impiety . . . instance be if fail bow down before justice . . . . But, oh, there be test and challenge and outcome . . ." he halt. "Where be I? Wait," hold up hand, "tell not. Yes, yes. When Goggler blaspheme and serve in jail and come out jail and still not respect King of Goggler who put he in jail, he be out of mind; complete and hopeless insane, and these Goggler be crazy!"

Most delegate not hear or listen. These talk one to other and shout across aisle . . . some play with other or self. Few delegate attend what said or what go on.

Hoora bang gavel on podium.

77

"Goggler! Goggler! We stand adjourn for two hour. When return we complete argue."

Gavel bang again and delegates jump from seat with roar. Quick these mix, slapp back, shake hand and hugg. Animal spirit take turn do handspring and somersault. Several kick friend, fist fight start and general melee, but slowly hall empty and when no spectator left, fighter stop fight and walk out arm in arm.

In two-hour wait, I make close acquaint Cuddle. Then delegate back in seat and Hoora on dais, pound gavel.

He turn to Professor. "Professor! Continue!"

Professor bow grave. "Did not old Majority decide when be no basis for determine?" He wait to be asked, then demand irascible, "Ask! Ask!"

Senator with two hat rise and ask, "Professor, need determine we be paranut and these be all right?"

Professor meditate before reply. "Be difficult question Senator, and not know I can answer." While convention wait, Professor stroke beard and study problem. Final say, "No. Not. Be no reason decide that. We act in way these did think queer. We talk in way these not talk, and so these decide we be crazy."

Irregular voice run loud, but end of sentence drop to whisper. With sudden turn raise voice to loud and strong and Professor strike air forceful with fist to give word.

"Now! Now! Since standard establish with no right, let we make these stand to measure!" Voice fall to firm and even tone as add, "To we . . . conservative act queer, and these talk queer. Be enough. These depart from conduct expect of Goggler. Mania, demania, remainia, or memania, these be not us, therefore these be not normal."

Cheer shake hall. Delegates stamp and whistle and march. Here and there delegate smash article on nearest head while other individual cry copious and tear hair, and still other sit in place and laugh. Not all delegate active. Be those maintain dignity by sitt in place and nodd to neighbor; and most great number, sit still face blank, show nothing.

Hoora bang gavel but take long time to quiet crowd. Hoora thunder, "Quiet! I preside here! I be Chair!" Eye flash. He glare challenge at any who dispute. All perfect still, he speak to Senator with two hat.

"Senator?"

"Yes, Goggler. These in Old Majority, especial in White District from which I come and which I represent, say us crazy. Well . . . maybe some of thee are," cheer of crowd turn to boos but Senator continue, "but when these say we be all crazy that be crazy." Crowd swing from boo to cheer again. Senator add, "When these say I be crazy, I . . ." he hesitate and turn slow, stress dignity, then finish, "that be too much. I . . . me . . . one of most sane and smart in world . . . crazy?"

As he halt, convention be proper impress, out of spirit and air, chant rise and grow to great and great proportion as more delegate take up.

"Crazy! Crazy! He crazy, I crazy!"

Hoora join chorus and all sing. Above wave of sound, Senator voice be heard shrill and penetrate, "Hahahaha, hahahahahahahahahah, thee be all crazy." Laugh like trumpet cut through noise 'til Senator led out. Crowd stop chant and Chair bang gavel.

"I Chair! I ask question. We say these be crazy. But this be convention. Let every have say. I decide." Pouting, he refuse to look at delegate, then satisfy, urge crowd.

"Delegate! Need settle business. Let we go."

Casanova Detro, spokesgoggler for delegate from Pinks shreik, "Let talk! I want talk!"

Hair sleek down in line with dark eyebrow that accent eye deep and black. Face be combine of handsome, pretty, and good-looking. Hoora turn to Casanova. "Man-of-world have floor."

Detro rise, rubb hand, light face to look like Satyr. Feet tap dance on floor and convention respond with cheer, laugh, applause and whistle. Few stand and dance too. Detro hand shoot forward in supplicate as he shout.

"Love! That be! Love and sex and good time. That what want! That what always want. These not free us. Of course," he smirk sly, "we get little. But we not free . . . what mean that? Be no crazy for that? I ask!"

It be rhetoric question and Detro continue with speech. "I re-

79

member when I be in love, feel good. I so happy, feel not bad. I think Goggle beautiful and Goggler great. Fruit be meal. Need not clothes. Need not any but love.

"Then Goggler hear how happy I be and start talk. Say I have mania. Ask what of love know I? I not care. I explain I want nothing differ. Tell these about love and these say know love. But what love? What bring? Look what it do to Goggler. It trouble. These said these love, but spoil life. What say I? I say satisfy love and happy, not ask question. These say I crazy! I say, okay, crazy. But let all be like I be."

To delegate he demand, "Be I crazy? No! No! Thousand time No!"

Hand in air emphasize word. Abrupt Casanova start jig and sing. Abrupt as start, he stop.

"Still like love. I think these be crazy spoil it. These be crazy! These be crazy!"

He repeat words 'til he pick up tune of early chant and dance. Convention catch fever and place sweep with song and noise and dance. Hoora after sing first ten minute, pound gavel.

"Delegate! Delegate! I be Chair! Quiet! Quiet!"

After twenty minute commotion, noise stop.

Delegate shriek, "Let be! Let we show these though these be crazy we leave alone to do what like long as commit no crime or violate no law. No special treat because these crazy. No put in jail when do nothing! And no leave free when commit crime! I say let these free like we. What say you? Free! Free! Free! Free!"

Convention begin new chant, "Free! Free! Free!" Hoora pound gavel again. "Wait for me. I Chair!"

As stern Chair he frown, puff chest out and strut up and down behind stand. When hall quiet, Hoora lower eyebrow, hunch shoulders and announce, "Floor open for further discuss."

Representative from Hall round Justice raise hand. All lawyer in group be prodd and urge. "Object! Go on, object! Take except! Respectful object! Object respectful! Fight these. Oppose these."

"Mr. Chair." Legal Eagle, manner fierce, seek right to speak. Hoora announce in loud voice, "Chair recognize Speaker from Hall round Justice!"

Judge slow evolve argue. "Be too easy say old Majority be insane because these did establish precedent by hold we not sane when we Minority. But we be circumspect and careful when thing be easy. Reason Goggler, reason so."

He pause to let common Goggler catch profundis of argument.

"Remember. Yes," he shake finger in warn, "remember. We never agree we be non compos mentis because conduct be different from Old Majority. As consider and judge fact, bear in mind: if New Majority be sane because Majority, and therefore ipso facto, New Minority be insane, then need reverse early opine. Decree find also insane when we in Minority.

"Be so? Of sure not! We always be sane. Therefore," he stick index finger at heaven and make hand tremble to argue strong, "therefore, insist we alway sane when in Minority, we need agree New Minority not be in insane condition!"

From gallery delegate shout, "What about we?"

"Ah," Legal Eagle point finger in direction of voice. "Ah!" He pause so word "ah" make impression, then finish. "If New Minority be not insane because differ than New Majority, conclusion be," he look about "we be all insane!"

When Judge sit down, friend and co-delegate slap on back and congratulate he.

Hoora stand before stand, deep think.

"Now," he say, "you say these be crazy. We must decide still other question. Since now Minority never be call crazy, what be group want be like us? Siketrist here," he indicate a fellow with smile that look natural in gathering and explain, "he be one of New Minority. He be good to me and now want be one of we. Should we hear?" Without wait reply, Hoora wave go ahead to Siketrist.

"Your Excellence!" Hoora bow, gleam of pride in eye. He wave hand in benedict to doctor to continue.

"Your Excellence, and Goggglers. These who wish be of thy group, though never be before, be borderline case. These be class alway report as increase in insane. One year or two, these be new addition. Be unfair to deprive these now of stand which achieve in time."

Most convention delegate nod in agree and stamp and shout of approve. Siketrist continue. "Take self. Borderline often think be crazy. I be more loose nut than tight. I say, 'I be damn'. I say, 'I guess everyone out of mind but self,' and then laugh, and add, 'or vice-versa.' Thee see I borderline and be one of thee. Beside," he bend forward sly, "thee need treat Goggler in other group."

Convention roar approve. Hoora quiet these and demand, "Who else?"

Legal Eagle rise. "Mr. Chair. I move we send conservative minority to sanatorium as these sent we. In fact," he nod to self in agree with own thought, "we shud send these to jail. Yes," he become excit, "I like. Let send these to jail."

"But Mr. Chair," Siketrist intervene, "Goggler from Hall round Justice argue only minute back these not insane. Now he say we send these to jail. Be not consistent."

"What?" Judge shriek. "Me not consistent? Thee be contempt. Send thee to jail!" He see sudden light. "Beside, since these not crazy, new injustice it be to say we be crazy. That point. We send these to jail."

Convention take up new chant and sing, "Send to jail, send to jail." Goggler follow Judge and march in tune with chant, sing, shout, walk, cry, crawl, bawl, brawl, and maul, down to asylum where these surrender self accord with Logg rule these remain in asylum 'til date of election.

I write no more. Convention be good exercise for radical. Let Gogg be who Gogg be—I be King and Sire.

Having writ these events down in case other follow I who read language of country. I teach Goggler to speak my tongue, but not teach these read or write. These be slow to learn. Have too few year for learn, and be not wise for teach these too much. If be say by who follow in future, I did not enough for Goggler, in reply I say I teach these much, and this be some of what I give.

1. I teach these assimmolate and how be refine with not so much hair and with wear of clothes; and these get breast on female.

2. I teach true democrazy, except for control I keep as King.

3. Teach democrazy in choose candidate and in hold politic convention and in right of all to speak.

4. I teach Goggler how have and use House of Lords, I call Logg—Court.

5. I set rule absolute right of majority—and right of each vote—always subect right of I, Peter, King and Father of every Goggler.

Part III

DEMOCRAZY: THE SELECTIVE
PROCESS

FOR SOME TIME Longfellow sat in the chair holding the book on his lap, thinking that Peter One had been the devil incarnate. His own determination to conduct himself righteously with these people was steeled by the report. Jenkins had been an ungodly seeker of personal satisfaction and pleasures. He had given no thought for the best interests of the Gogglers. Adultery had been the prime order of Peter One's principles, and the people, instead of being properly outraged, had loved him. Longfellow could tell that by their adoration and imitation. Well, he would not abuse and take advantage of their simplicity. He would do only what was right and teach them the right kind of love. His outrage and the need for more rest left him weary, and he lay down and slept a while. When he awakened, he washed his face and changed into a fresh suit which had been laid out for him. He descended to the lower room where the doctor was waiting.

"It be time," said the host. "Better we hurry or be late for Gogg."

There was no sound between them as they hurried along. This gave Longfellow an opportunity to try and organize the many

84

thoughts that flowed through his mind in constant eddying disturbances. He had seen and heard some remarkable things. There were elements of confusion—dizziness.

Suddenly the doctor broke his thoughts. "Here be."

Fifty feet away was the Gogg's cave. Longfellow felt the lawyer tug his jacket. "Leave thee here. I have appoint and not stay."

Longfellow watched Perceiver move off, glad that he would be alone with the Gogg. The doctor had not arranged to call for him, which might mean that he expected his night would be spent at the Gogg's home.

Longfellow shrugged. The road was separated from the pedestrian walk by a narrow gully and he walked along the gully until he was in front of the entrance. His eye had already examined the front. It was a mound of stone approximately one hundred yards all around. It appeared to be a solid white teardrop from an erupting volcano which on his closer inspection proved to be ground stone, ground shells or ground volcanic ash. A design in spirals was formed wherever two sections of stone met—a design created by a running color like the black of mussels. On the top and in the walls were statues, all very similar, which he later learned were likenesses of Peter One.

Following the curved path which led into the house, Longfellow was met by the young man of that afternoon, who once again flipped in obeisance, and then without a word or sign led him into a foyer of immense proportions. Waiting in the foyer at the usher's sign, Longfellow scanned the walls hung with hand painted pictures of different Gogglers which he assumed were past Goggs. There was none of the incumbent Gogg; but every third one, from its looks, had to be of Peter One. He guessed it was the custom to hang ex-Goggs in this foyer and that Peter One insisted on his importance frequently.

The Gogg came out bowing, hand extended in greeting.

"Wait thee. Family out but be home in short time and be distress when learn thee here and they not." His apology flowed on without pause, "Be home in short."

"Let we go in." Taking Longfellow's arm he guided him into a large dining hall where a table was set with food. Longfellow sat down as directed. The Gogg sat down also, unfolded a napkin and started his meal. A small female Goggler served them and during the entire meal not a word was spoken by the Gogg. Longfellow followed his example.

After they had finished their dinner, the Gogg, still without a word, in a half bandy-legged walk, led him to a narrow and long corridor-like space. There were chairs and holes in the wall which looked to the outside. With a slight stretch of the imagination the space he was in could be considered a patio. At the far end stood a large white stone statue. Longfellow walked over and studied it. The lines and the art were excellent—a full length woman too slender and delicate for a Goggler. Longfellow was impressed by the sculptor's vision or hope for the future of the Gogglers.

"Imagine piece by most great sculptor," the Gogg told him. "Notice thee, example culture and great advance civilize. Sculptor conceive as model of more assimmolate." Longfellow gazed at the concept of what further assimmolation would do for the Gogglers. It was a visionary piece. The woman had been given long slender legs, shapely but not heavy thighs, a sylphic torso with smoothly rounded hips. Above her slim waist and slenderized body, the bust stood out large and conspicuous. Gogglers in reality were squat and muscular, with thighs of great power and strength. The statue anticipated the coming of others—the offspring of Peter One by many years.

As the Gogg and Longfellow sat talking, a woman came into the patio from the dining room. She was the first Goggler Longfellow had seen with red hair. She flowed across the patio toward them with unexpected grace, her walk accenting her hips. The lumbering gait which raised first one shoulder then another, so noticeable in the other Gogglers, was missing. From her manner, her bearing, and the richness of her accoutrements, Longfellow concluded it could be no one but the Gogg's wife. Glistening green eyes sparkled against the background of her red hair. Despite the long arms and flat face she was an attractive woman and her full-bosomed show of descent from Peter One made her easy to look at. Longfellow loved redheads.

She came up to them, and waited almost primly for the Gogg

Longfellow gazed at the concept of what further assimmdation would do for the Gogglers. It was a visionary piece. The woman had been given long slender legs, shapely but not heavy thighs, a sylphic torso with smoothly rounded hips.

to make the first sign. For a few moments the two stood there in tableau. It was almost as if it was calculated to impress him and make him see why he should aid them to greater culture.

"O Dram." The Gogg gestured to his wife.

"How do you do?" Longfellow responded respectfully, impressed by her looks and manner, uncertain of what might come next, sort of standing on tiptoe, knowing she was a Goggler. Expectantly, almost gingerly, he waited for their lead, for this was not an everyday situation. His righteous sense of propriety had not disappeared, but it was not quite so righteous as it had been before. At home he would not have looked at O Dram.

While he waited for their move or word, she bowed slightly, her breasts swaying gently in his direction, and her "How be dinner?" came in a deep but full and warm voice.

"Very nice, thank you" he replied, still formal and polite, still remaining tentative and watchful.

To relax the atmosphere she said, "Hope see thee most often. Be sorry, be so. . . . "

Longfellow raised his hand to interrupt her. "Don't explain, please." His eyes spoke also as he said, "It was quite all right, and I'll give you plenty of opportunity to entertain me." With such as she around he began to wonder if he could stay out of the trees.

The tension eased and they both smiled.

"Can get water?" she asked.

Longfellow accepted the offer with alacrity.

Both men turned and watched her walk the length of the patio, feet going slightly outward as her hips swayed.

Longfellow cleared his throat. "Charming woman, your wife."

The Gogg beamed. "Thank thee. Thank much. Perhaps thee honor with . . . aid further assimmolate. As see, O Dram be one of most high bred Peter on Goggle."

Longfellow's difficulty with Perceiver the night before remained in his mind. If he tried to separate the two parts of what the Gogg said, the Gogg would think he meant to challenge the statement that O Dram was one of the best bred . . . or that he didn't think well of her . . . or that he didn't like her. If he denied

88

his willingness to aid in the family's assimmolation it might be nothing but argument, and this, after all, was the Gogg. Later, when the time was right, he could make his refusal. Agreeably he said "Yes, I can see that."

"You said these, when you spoke of your family . . . are there other members?" Longfellow inquired.

"Sister. In room. This night not like thee meet too many, be strain know too many."

"Yes. You are a wise man." Longfellow allowed his eyes to return to the figure of the statue. At least there was no danger of offending by a too close look. Yet, since studying the stone figure was studying art, why was it any less the study of art to study the real figure for which the statue was modeled? The pleasure of watching the beautiful way O Dram had of walking flowed over Longfellow as she brought him the water. The three of them talked at random about many topics, but no one mentioned assimmolation. Finally, unable to hide his weariness, Longfellow yawned.

"Excuse me."

The Gogg and his wife were profuse in their apologies for keeping him up so long. All rose and went from the patio into the house. Longfellow was extremely tired. His ordeal of three weeks, hoping but not believing in rescue, was not easily relaxed by one night's sleep. Without thinking, he said, "I'm so worn out I almost wish someone would put me to bed."

All the way to the room which had been set apart for him, he kept yawning. Without being told, he could see that the room had special meaning and feeling. The pictures on the wall, the magnificent but formal bed, and the elegance of all the furniture fostered this belief. The Gogg said, "Peter One sleep here."

Longfellow tried the bed with his hand, sat on it and finding it soft, with a great sigh stretched his arms back.

"Goodnight," said the Gogg and before Longfellow or O Dram could respond, closed the door behind him.

Longfellow was not really surprised at the Gogg's leaving, although he hadn't expected to be performing the obligations of a husband, for in his own mind he had determined that this behavior in the present circumstances was criminal—even improper. The doctor had first talked to him about assimmolation, and he expected the Gogg would too, if he were going to ask this sinful conduct. O Dram, a Peter, with full breasts exposed and framed by her breastplate walked to the bed and sat down by his side waiting for instructions.

"Do you not feel embarrassed, alone here in a bedroom with a strange man?"

"Embarrass I be, though did meet downstairs. Embarrass I be to ask thee serve." A quaint look was on her face. "Please tell what do; how act."

"My dear O Dram." Longfellow fumbled his lines, thinking he knew what to say next but finding himself unable to say it. "Did your husband instruct you to stay here with me? Did he tell you to have me perform a . . . a . . . service?"

"Yes Sire. But I never with other than Gogg, and be without know what to do. Please tell how act."

"Act? You should be indignant. Your life is with the Gogg. Any physical contact with another man, myself or any man, is sinful. God will punish you . . . and myself as well. Such conduct is a violation of good morals, good ethics, good conduct, and even good wifery."

O Dram studied Longfellow with a look of disbelief on her face. "Be not what Peter One teach? Peter One teach other with advance culture assimmolate 'til breed improve and all like thee. Not correct?"

"No. I mean I don't know about the breeding part of it. But just having sex violates all the decent tenets of my moral code. It is sinful and should only be indulged in between husband and wife."

"Thee like not I? Not good carry for assimmolate?"

"Oh no. There's nothing personal about it. It's just that it's irreligious; it's sinful; it's improper; don't you understand?"

O Dram moved to get off the bed. "If I be repulsive, I go. Seek not assimmolate so much force serve." Tears slowly formed in her eyes and they brimmed over.

Longfellow put his hand on her shoulder. "Wait, please. I

must make you understand." O Dram sobbed, put her head on his chest, and her hand on his leg to support herself. He carefully removed her hand. The loss of support caused her to fall over in his direction, and the added weight brought them both to a reclining position. Her tears had run down her face to her bosom, and Longfellow took out his handkerchief and tried to dry them.

"Understand," he told her, still trying to stop her tears, "there is nothing personal about my objections. As a matter of fact you are most attractive, and one of the most desirable women I've met."

As she turned to him to listen, her breasts leaned out of her breastplate and touched his chin as he talked. The lower part of her body had fallen over him, and they remained pressed together as she sobbed, allowing her tears to run freely. He reached up in an effort to push her breasts aside but they swung back to his face and the weight of her body on his kept him from getting up or moving. Between her sobs, her voice filled deeply with a different emotion and Longfellow, though intending to avoid what was coming found he was unable to resist. He tried again to wipe away her tears, touching them wherever they ran, but the firmer his resolve the more his resistance faded until he accepted what was unavoidable. In a few seconds he was nude.

They lay talking an hour later and she told him, "Gogg be envy of thee." She caressed him. "This be amaze. Why not wish join I? Be not attract thee?"

"I've told you that you are very attractive." Holding her where he had found her firm and soft, he still urged his droll point of view. "But it is a sin in our religion and in our living for a woman to have physical relations with a man to whom she isn't married. And when one of the two is married to another it compounds the sin. We must never do this again."

"What be sin?"

"Sin? It is the greatest of evils. Like adultery. That's when a married person has sex with a person other than his or her spouse. The Bible says this is one of the great sins."

"But what be sin?"

Longfellow looked at her as if he thought she was suggesting he didn't know what he was talking about, but it was evident she was innocently sincere. What was sin, he cogitated. After a moment's thought during which he still held her, he attempted to answer.

"Well, for one thing it is going against law or custom. Sometimes the law is divine and sometimes it is made by man."

She interrupted, "If make by man, man can take away. Gogg make law . . . but not sin law."

Two fingers on her mouth stopped her talking and Longfellow resumed his explanation.

"It's not only violating a man-made rule . . . it's violating a rule of God . . . it's a wickedness . . . depravity." Even while he said it, he knew she didn't understand him or the words . . . and, as he feared, she asked the question he knew would be too difficult to answer.

"Rule of God? What be? What be God?"

"God? God is the supreme being who created and rules the whole Universe."

"Be more supreme than Peter?"

"Oh yes. More than the whole world."

"More big than Peter?"

"Of course. Bigger than everything."

The questions seemed mocking but he knew she was sincere and couldn't be mocking him, even though she expressed her doubts when she asked.

"If God bigger than every . . . make every . . . control every . . . why sin to . . . make more better child . . . make not sin."

She talked so innocently. He took his hand from her mouth and replaced it on her breasts which had quivered whenever she talked. It disturbed him. When he held them he could not see them and he hoped by this method to quiet the stirrings they created. But the effect he had hoped for within himself was contradicted as he felt the quickening pulse beat within his stomach. At the same time the pulse of O Dram sped up his fingers and her voice caressed him.

"Be more sin, we here and sin over?"

"Of course," he insisted. But he did not move away from her, for this would hurt her feelings.

"But husband not mind. In true, he consider thee render favor to he. Be most good of thee."

Longfellow railed at himself as he cooperated, "I am very weak. I must expiate my sin sometime."

Next morning, considerably refreshed, Longfellow awakened to find the sun had been up a few hours. He touched a bell by the side of the bed as he had been instructed. In a few minutes everything he needed was brought to him. He washed and dressed and went downstairs.

At breakfast with the Gogg and O Dram, he thought the Gogg glanced at him surreptitiously as though he were studying him. Nothing was said about the night before and shortly after breakfast when Longfellow was leaving to return to the doctor's house, the Gogg said, "Come more."

O Dram smiled and walked with him to the exit.

"Didst thou mean about sin and not assimmolate?"

"Of course."

"Did realize, I be leave thee pure. Have nice day." A few steps away from the door she turned back, a plea in her eyes and voice, "Please come more."

Gogglers were all around the doctor's cave as Longfellow approached and the doctor came out to him. "Welcome, Sire!" said the doctor leading him through the rear entrance. As soon as they had stepped inside the door, the doctor burst forth.

"People come great many. Rich, important, middle class, poor. All want assimmolate. Make demand as wish."

"Doctor, I've told you that what they want . . . what you all want . . . is sinful, and I will not be a party to it."

"Yes. Know what tell. But rich not many. Important not many."

"Very well. We will discuss this at another time. Now I am returning to the Gogg's house . . . if you don't mind."

Perceiver looked at Longfellow as if he expected an explanation, but Longfellow did not respond.

93

Perceiver walked to the Gogg's place with him. They arrived only to learn neither the Gogg nor O Dram were at home. Longfellow realized his good intentions would have to wait for a more propitious time.

Walking away from the Gogg's place a short distance, he and the doctor came upon another white stone edifice of more imposing architecture. Perceiver waved his hand toward it.

"Here have protector of liberty and fountain of justice; all law be interpret."

In his manner there was none of the humility that he had exhibited in speaking of Longfellow's country, and Longfellow knew he was speaking of the Goggler Supreme Court.

"But," wondered Longfellow out loud, "since the Gogg makes the law, could not the Gogg clear up any question?"

"Oh, no. Function of Court interpret law. Function of Gogg make law. If Gogg also interpret . . . no need court, national calamity; and if Gogg misinterpret law extend power. Many question of law not question of law."

The doctor-attorney waxed eloquent. "Even now great question before Court."

Without waiting for Longfellow to show interest, he plunged into the details. "Citizen sue, demand Loggic declare Gogg not most bigg. Citizen offer proof of actual measure that other more big."

"A challenging argument," Longfellow admitted. "It would be interesting to know how the court handles the subject."

While talking they had walked the full length of the street to the entrance of the structure which housed the Court. It was an interesting square stone formation with statues on top, in front and around it. Longfellow noticed with great amusement that all were of the same person—Peter One. Inside, they walked through vaulted corridors and the severity of the architectural lines of the walls and ceiling imposed a stillness which spread over the halls.

"Is the Gogg opposing the suit?" Longfellow inquired.

"Natural. Gogg vindicate self and oppose change. Custom

94

It was an interesting square stone formation with statues on top, in front and around it. Longfellow noticed with great amusement that all were of the same person – Peter One.

base of law, customtution law backbone society," he made a deferential obeisance to Longfellow, "as Peter One lay out."

Longfellow thought he detected implications in what the lawyer said. "Why do you say it that way? What has happened so far?"

The lawyer struggled with a seeming reluctance. "Gogg claim time of select over; thing of past; Court have not right inquire. Question be argue now."

Just then they reached a massive, almost square opening with stone doors that swung back easily onto a lofty and large room. The air of the place was thin and chilled with austerity, and an aura of sanctity weighed down upon them. Longfellow, impressed, dropped into a vacant seat near the rear of the room.

Gogglers were swarming through the room—just like in Peter One's day. Perceiver pointed to a fellow down front at the counsel table.

"That be Pompos. Be customtution lawyer, profound thinker; president all bank and wealthy rich."

Longfellow noticed that Pompos was of medium height and boasted a girth that made the remaining members of his troupe look thin, a build emphasized by his lack of a neck and short bandy legs. His features, clearly bearing anthropoid characteristics, were thick and his face broad.

"Hrrmph!" Pompos said in a deep voice of authority, while he seated himself at the middle of the counsel table, cheeks puffing full and empty, like a bellows at work.

Coming after him and seating themselves consecutively were three lawyers of clear definition.

"That," said Longfellow's informer, indicating the one next to Pompos, a tall thin Goggler whose face was pressed in at the sides and whose clothes hung loosely over him like a seamless bundle of cloth, "be Pimpas. Next come Muddle and last, Meddle."

The latter two were of medium height, not marked by any outstanding characteristic of personality or feature. All four lawyers wore hats, but their big feet had no shoes. Longfellow abandoned his scrutiny of them to watch the continuing group that filed in.

"First man of lead group, be Upright. From old family," Perceiver pointed.

Longfellow saw a tall and broad-shouldered Goggler, his stature exaggerated by a military bearing. At no time did Upright relax his shoulders or the constant outward curve of his chest or the permanent hard line of his chin. The hair on his head and face was so prominent, despite the hat he wore, that he looked rather closely like a descendant of a gorilla tribe. He sat at the counsel table next to Pompos. Upright's three associates had filed in behind him and sat at the table on the side closest the door through which they had come. The first after Upright, was tall, affecting dignity, his importance heightened by a shock of white hair which curled out of the sides of his hat.

"White hair be Downright, one of most pure blood Peter on Goggle. Great culture and civilize. Unfortunate . . . wife never have child . . . shame for such cut off." The legal one nudged Longfellow. "Other two be Twaddle and Twiddle."

Longfellow smiled. The names were inherited, no doubt. Peter One had planned his fun for generations to come—so he could look up and laugh.

A rising curtain up front revealed thirteen judges sitting behind a bench formed and shaped in triangles that crossed the room like building blocks. Each triangle had a judge behind it. If one were to lay dominoes across each other, with the end afoul against the side of another and the side against the end of the next, the design would resemble the bench as he saw it. Now Longfellow could understand the description Peter One had attempted in his manuscript.

The Chief Judge, Popoff, descendant of the original great judge from Peter One's time looked exactly like his forebears, as Perceiver explained, even to the wig he wore. As custom required, and as Longfellow recalled from Peter One's tome, the wigs were bald with curls on the lower edges, around the ears and on the back of the neck.

All the other Judges faced backwards with wigs down to their shoulders on which there were painted faces on the audience side. Their chairs were so designed that they might support the head

97

without hiding the wig face. Longfellow was tickled to see that the faces on the wigs resembled the faces of the judges that wore them.

Perceiver explained further, "Custom Goggle since first day Court. Old member know old rule and tradition . . . look front. New judge not vote new law. Look back at old law for instruct and guide."

"Popoff?"

"Oh, Popoff old judge."

Just then the Clerk, a hairy and stentorian-voiced Goggler, held up his hand and proclaimed, "Court be."

Popoff nodded to the barristers and the twelve other Loggicers nodded shortly after in unison.

Pompos spoke first. "Thine Honor and gentlemen of law. Action by citizen ask Court say Gogg not most big on Goggle when select; and not entitle Gogg; and not now Gogg; and Gogg not Gogg."

Pompos, his voice a deep throaty grind, continued, his right arm raised in a gesture directing the Court's attention to the right corner of the ceiling.

"As all citizen know, select Gogg for most big on Goggle. Honors," his nodding head slowly turned so that each Judge had at least a short acknowledgement, "when say most big, not mean Goggler think most big; or most big if other not. Nor most big by mistake, or most big by Gogg."

He pronounced the words in rhythm, and the rhyming brought forth a smile upon the otherwise dour countenance of Popoff.

"Honor," the voice rose to a rasp, "when say most big, mean most big. Proof be show, on day of select of Dram, other on Goggle inch more big and should be Gogg. Proof show on day of select, measure of Gogg Dram and measure of other citizen. Measure show clear Gogg not Gogg and not be Gogg."

Pompos stopped talking and Muddle began.

"Honor. Great reward to I permit in case which control future of Goggle, and politic system. Never in history such challenge. Never in history any Goggler suggest Gogg be not most big.

Before Honor Court, if Gogg most big now, not point. Point be, be Gogg most big day of select?

"For ordinary mind, ordinary Goggler to break tradition be beyond character, beyond strength. Must need recognize, Loggicers for Goggle and govern of Goggle, follow only rule law and custom. Custom be so firm only most great dare change. Only most great as Honor."

Muddle twisted, his head going forward as he bent from the waist. He directed his words to Popoff.

"Great man be rare and when be, seldom be . . . and so say to Honor . . . genius break tradition which be inculcate in he and all forebear since beginning justice time."

Great emphasis was laid on the words "justice time," but at this point Muddle seemed to have forgotten his thought for when he sought to resume the thread of his argument, he was lost, his eyes blinked and their lashless lids accentuated the baldness of the front of his face.

"Ah!" There was a paen of delight in his recovery of his theme. "Some people retain free spirit while subject self to great weight custom. To such, change be nature. Young like change occasional . . . and be compatible with live. Age, on other hand, already pass change and set."

His mind wandered again for a moment, but his face lit as he remembered. "Ah, change. Variety Spice life."

"Hrrrmmmppp," Pompos remarked and Muddle was startled into a flurry of words.

"Ordinary Goggler who change custom after ripe age tear root; root be lost when try crawl in new niche."

Popoff moved his head up and down slowly and looked at Muddle and asked, "Realize not pretend young? Be man of my age."

"Yes, Honor," Meddle jumped up and down and Muddle's voice stopped. "Honor man of age but man of vision. Man who lead to change and be exception who make rule. Disregard of year, Honor alway be young. Philosopy change. Young and old refer to mind and spirit, not body. Age or young be test average. Men like Honor . . . ."

99

Perceiver bent over to Longfellow derisively. "Popoff never deviate rule or custom."

Meddle's voice flowed on. " . . . spirit alway subject great unrest; ever stir to new high fly crusade for thing . . . or change."

Pompos slapped his hand upon the table with a resounding thwack, and Meddle quieted. Pompos pushed his voice up. He was not to be denied the most prominent part in the presentation of this great philosophical problem.

"Honor, true great find self beset by constant inner question and quest; critical faculty always weigh and measure thing which but recent seem absolute. Young lack change quality, or age lack change quality not so much settle body as mind. Settle be satisfy. We not satisfy as be. Content, abundant, not enough for critical faculty. Different be necessary to grow, and to change customtution be right. Urge take testament witness who swear that at time select, Gogg not be most big."

As the members of the firm of Pompos, Pimpas, Muddle and Meddle sat down, the opposing four barristers rose together in chorus.

Upright, as the head of the firm, made the opening address.

"Honor, we for Gogg speak, and for Goggler speak, say present action be outrage. Not only do case offend Gogg, and be outside measure season, but comment derogatory in violate most fundament principle of Goggle; action pull down most sacred article which history and govern be base; to wit and whereas, great Goggle-eye. Goggle-eye do say Gogg most big."

Downright took up the argument.

"Examine law, which be fact. In free select period, day and night and week and month, Goggle measure contender."

"And what use for measure, except naked eye?" challenge Pimpas from the side.

"Measure?" Twiddle made reply. "Measure say? All measure and device for measure. Ruler, cord, hand span, foolstick, any . . . every device. I tell not how done. Familiar method, use many time. Plus, alway relative . . . compare and measure."

"Ah," said Pimpas. "There be rub. Relative . . . compare.

Compare be odious? Theory of compare, challenge select. Tell . . .
tell Court . . . how do? When Goggler give opportunity?"

Here Upright seized the issue.

"Examine better when candidate in public. Goggler swarm
over and measure with all measure. Candidate show self for measure. Alway prostrate in select period."

"But relative? Issue be void. Question be beg."

"Additional measure method. Who study anatomy know bone
of body definite have relate in size. Small bone exact relation
large bone. Some measure feet, some other member, some organ,
and some measure mouth, and make determination. Goggler . . .
by use one part anatomy or other, determine size of whole."

At the end of this explanation of the theory of relativity, one
of the twelve reversed Loggicers so far forgot himself as to turn
around and look startled.

Downright resumed his flow of unction. "Honor. Why action
brought? Not to put Gogg out for present. Ten year term most
done. What for action? Claim to end incumbentcy. If look at facts
close, purpose be discredit great Dram so Goggler not select he
again. And when do other bring case? On day of begin free talk
period so create doubt in mind Goggler. And who do? Pompos
do, who fancy self of most high culture and civilize and believe
self should be Gogg. Discredit Gogg so Goggler turn to he as who
reduce Gogg."

"Conspiracy more." The sound was still Downright.

"Predicate theory once court lean gainst Gogg he withdraw.
Why? Simple. Goggle-eye select, which these attack today but
defend next week. Most firm be in see candidate. Goggler have to
measure he, where Goggler never see candidate have not opportunity to measure. Full bench of Court be compel so say, for be fundamental. More likely Goggler refuse select, because so great
respect tradition."

At this point, Pompos chiseled into the discussion to rebut.
"Talk of Goggle-eye and certainty it be pure nosense. Vaunted
Goggle-eye often blur."

He sneered at the thought, then became serious again in such
a way as to suggest that one like himself should be selected.

"Satisfy need of Goggler large void to fill. Yet," he waited to let the importance of the observation sink in, "if remain most tiny bit not fill, one seek to fill. However big Gogg, be hope and desire for more big."

First Pompos, Pimpas, Muddle and Meddle, then Upright, Downright, Twaddle and Twiddle sat down, and while all the lawyers, counselors, attorneys, solicitors, advocates and barristers remained seated, the thirteen members of the Logg arose and filed out. They were hardly out of the door when the Clerk rapped, and they turned and began to file back in. Longfellow was startled to discover the twelve incumbent Gogg appointees going through a transformation. They removed their reverse masks and put on bald forward looking wigs. When they were all seated, Popoff cleared his throat and his voice came out faltering.

"Unanimous opine of Court. Be ask set to side customtution practice and guarantee. Be ask declare rule Goggle-eye supremacy not supreme. Be ask substitute court decide, for that of Goggler. We not do; nor will. If petitioner appeal because incumbent Gogg not all he believe, petitioner must present appeal to Goggler. Court find right to opine be absolute in Goggle-eye of Goggler, and Court have not right of over impose opine on Goggler. Clear to all citizen Goggle, and Court take judicial notice, measure must be take by these who vote. Not Court province to order one type of measure over other. Goggler use rod, or relative theory, or just bare Goggle-eye. One Goggler opine be one Goggler opine, and more than one Goggler opine be more than one Goggler opine; but majority opine be law. Be absolute. Be sine qua non and res ipsa loquitor, as great and belove forbear Peter did say. Once majority Goggler give opine which one be most big and he become Gogg no other measure could be.

"Petitioner argue opine base on see without measure. Not true. Not accurate. Not correct. If petitioner and/or one of witness use measure rod, he use eye to see mark on measure. Must use eye to see rule begin or end. Opine base on observe made by Goggle-eye. And no measure make with eye be more accurate. When collective eye of Goggle speak, be omnipotent. Be great pride that person with excellent eye be call Goggle-eye.

"Understand purpose of petitioner in file. Seek discredit for Gogg, to make retire. No Gogg be candidate, and Court rule he off ballot if not see in free three month period. If extend free period one second, then could be extend minute, then hour, then day, then month, then year, and then ten year. Make Gogg Gogg forever, destroy fundament rule for Goggle. Petition dismiss, unanimous."

Other Loggicers each nodded separately and consecutively, then all arose and left. The silence that followed was fraught with explosive potentialities as the barristers all arose and filed out in inverse order. Upright, Downright, Twaddle and Twiddle went first and were immediately followed by Pompos, Pimpas, Muddle and Meddle.

Those remaining in the room were decorous, but before a handful had left, the crowds, newly formed, set up a clamor outside. Longfellow and Perceiver hurried out to find the crowds cheering and marching up and down.

"Hurry," urged the lawyer. "If crowd see thee, never let go. If Logg know thee in Court, would suspend hear and give grand reception. Thee be great in demand."

"I did not know. Yes, I did know from this morning, and from what you told me, but I didn't know that even the Loggicers would be seeking me out," replied Longfellow.

The medico-lawyer smiled. "Thee can have from any. But not hurry. No hurry these to help I. Have few case pend and Logg member may seek out I to intercede for assimmolate and advance civilize."

Longfellow recognized the simple character of the Gogglers in that whatever he told them of his views and wishes with respect to assimmolation they still saw it from their own perspective. No physical contact meant no physical contact for someone else. Perhaps, since they were like children, and wished so much for cooperation and kindness from him, he would have to yield his inflexible principles. The provoking thought was the fruit of their pressure.

Without any explanation to Perceiver, he turned to try again at the Gogg's and see if O Dram had returned so he could resume his discussion with her; his parting from O Dram seemed more unfriendly in retrospect with each passing hour. Leaving Perceiver behind he found his way to the Gogg's where he was received by the Gogg with much pomp. Slightly embarrassed, he delayed his inquiry about O Dram and sat talking to the Gogg. He looked at the square torsoed Gogg and his mind returned to earlier events of the afternoon and the session of the Logg and he recalled he had not seen the Gogg there.

"Your Goggship, how was it that I didn't see you at the session of the Logg today?"

"I not attend unless be involve. If court inquire not further, not need be there."

Just then O Dram came in and sat down with them.

The Gogg seemed anxious that the subject of the lawsuit not be mentioned in her presence for immediately he told Longfellow, "Will think over for few day and advise?"

"What be that, Goggship?" O Dram asked.

"No thing. No thing. Small matter of govern in which Sire be expert." Here, a penchant for allowing the thought which he had proscribed to slip out appeared, for he took up the question of the day.

"Decision of Logg today only decide which not upset govern and destroy system. Now, see long windy campaign; measure out fight which go to end. Campaign already on. Tonight end quiet, and tomorrow Pompos open for be select as Gogg."

"Pompos," Longfellow asked?

"Yes. Be he."

Having become aware of Longfellow's presence on Goggle, the male Gogglers expressed their homage according to caste. Those of the lower class, as had Bulbo, did a flip-flop in greeting him; while the Peterasses, as the higher caste, expressed their respect by a genuflection in which they bowed in rocking fashion, bent at the waist, head down, rear pointing and arms swinging back and forth like rocking toys Longfellow had seen at home.

The females adopted other methods of showing their veneration and submission. The No-Peters turned their backs to Long-

THE GOGGLERS OFFERED THEMSELVES FOR HIS CHOICE.

fellow and bent forward in hope of assimmolation. This gesture of exposure to procreation would be maintained until Longfellow had passed and their hope of being assimmolated on that occasion passed with him. The Peterasses, as the higher caste, considered such gestures undignified. In making their advances they sat on their heels with knees akimbo, prepared to be tapped for acceptance by Longfellow.

Frequently and recurrently during this period Longfellow heard about the political campaign being waged and the progress in the selection of Gogg, but his own preoccupation was so great that his thoughts on that subject were disjointed and unconnected. Houses, homes, businesses and jewels had been thrown at his feet. The knowledge that he was on Goggle affected the Gogglers outlook, for, though the Gogg was still the Chief Magistrate, so sought after was Longfellow, that important and prominent persons on the planet frequently gave him gifts and offered their influence in his behalf in the hope of winning the assimmolation he had generally refused. They were sure the whole thing was a matter of price, and his services became extra rare and valuable.

The common run of Gogglers believed Longfellow's refusal to assimmolate the citizens was because Longfellow felt they were not good enough for him; and while he was respected and even feared, he became disliked. Discussions among the Gogglers frequently revolved around the difference between Peter One and Peter Two . . . the first remembered as beloved because he did things to everyone, and Peter Two disliked because he refused to do the same things to them. But all classes of Gogglers hoped and sought to be assimmolated by Longfellow.

One middle class Goggler, one day, seeing Longfellow on the street, after doing his flip-flop, became excited and talked and prayed but his speech was so jumbled Longfellow thought the Goggler was in trouble, and followed him into his cave. There, the fellow's wife, upon seeing Longfellow, quickly bowed forward to make herself available, and at the same time wiggled her rear. Longfellow started to leave the house but the Goggler got down on his knees and talked and prayed to him and gestured as though

SHE ATTEMPTED TO ENCOURAGE HIM TO ASSIMMOLATE HER.

he would show him something. While Longfellow watched, the Goggler got up, took out a tweezers, and began to pluck hairs which showed over the edge of his wife's garments.

"See, Sire, what be reduce to. Must look like assimmolate."

"I see," he told the Goggler, "that you are very proud and wish to be as good as all your neighbors."

The Goggler agreed. "Yes Sire. When alike, no one better and no one worse." Suddenly his face took on a sly look. "Unless thee grant boon, and we be better."

As they stood talking, the female took off her clothes and climbed on the bed. The man tried to help Longfellow remove his coat. "This be for proud. Other pluck and be satisfy."

Longfellow wasn't sure whether the male referred to the tweezers or the attempt to take off his coat. Adroitly, he avoided the assistance and left the house.

During the next four weeks the campaign between the Gogg and Pompos swirled and eddied; every now and again, Longfellow would see one of the candidates on the ground with many Gogglers over him measuring his claim to the Goggship. Sometimes long lines of Gogglers waited a turn at the measuring process with some in the line complaining that those ahead were taking too long—urging them to hurry and give others a chance.

Longfellow continued to reside with Perceiver, searching for no cave or den of his own, but though he lived with him, he avoided the doctor as much as possible lest Perceiver monopolize his attention. On the few occasions when he did see the lawyer-medico, that politico suggested Longfellow publicly endorse Pompos. As a result of this, Longfellow developed a mistrust of Perceiver but not of O Perceiver or Palpater. He managed to convince himself that his further services were necessary to make sure that the first assimmolation should take and the offspring be only his. He had seen the Gogg and O Dram on a number of occasions but because of the political tumult he had not slept over. His memory of O Dram, the most delightful of the females he knew on Goggle, stimulated a desire and a need to visit and thus it was one day that he found himself in the Gogg's residence. The household was busy. A number of Gogglers were rushing around talking to each other and discussing the campaign. As Longfellow stood there the Gogg hurried to greet him and O Dram followed shortly. Longfellow remembered how well he liked her.

"Thee stay?" O Dram's question was part assurance and part plea. Longfellow agreed.

"Then," said O Dram, "allow to leave for little so can order right dinner and drink, and get self fix."

Tossing her head conquettishly at the end of the sentence, without waiting for Longfellow's consent, she marched off. Longfellow and the Gogg walked in the direction of the room where the ex-Goggs hung.

"How are things going, your Goggship?" Longfellow inquired.

"Not going. Campaign not develop as plan. Escape control; escape manage. All usual stimulant which build Gogg outstand have not effect." Distraction and despair were written on his Goggship's face.

"Day and day, legend of Pompos grow." His hope had little voice. "Slander, whisper, tell that I deprive people of full right, and break customtution law. Impossible fight. If say Pompos more deep, I do fight. I do fight; but not whisper."

The Gogg walked over to the window to watch the Gogglers pass, and Longfellow joined him. Neither spoke for a few minutes. "Your Goggship?" Longfellow broke the silence.

"Sire?"

"Pompos' lead is growing, isn't it?"

"It do so look." Though still despondent, Dram would not allow despair to destroy his philosophical point of view. "One grow in stature and look more large with people when constant project before. Vote for Gogg make feel more big; work show man at best, though take all out of he."

"But how do you explain Pompos' sudden strength?"

"Artificial. When I make campaign last, be support huge by contribute. Now, attack instead. Goggler of influence believe these could handle Pompos, but not handle I."

"How? Why?"

"New man offer thing new. Powerful Goggler back vote of Goggler and offer more. Repeater stand as before, add no thing to program already present. Successor extend self to present more than given. Stretch before Goggler great promise."

"Yes, that is true. But it's only a moment before people become accustomed to the new. You must admit that they will see you anew."

"If look for change, Pompos fresh and give more. If look back, not select I anyway."

For a while longer the two men stood gazing out of the window.

"I'm inclined to think that in the long run Pompos will be harder to handle than the Gogglers think . . . and more ruthless," commented Longfellow.

While standing at the window the Gogg saw someone entering. "Excuse, Sire. Clerk of Logg come. O Dram come here and entertain thee."

A sudden idea came to the Gogg and he stopped halfway in his approach to the door. "Like Sister visit thee?"

"No. Thank you very much. I'll wait until O Dram comes."

After the Gogg had left, Longfellow looked at his surroundings. His mind ran through an account of his conduct since he came to Goggle. Being alone is very much like facing your maker, he thought. It is a little bit of death, silent and overbearing; and according to one legend at least, when you face death your entire life sweeps before you. He realized that he had gone through the last month blithely receiving wealth without twice thinking that he had any obligation to the Gogglers, or evaluating them, their impressions, history and emotions. He had taken the numerous benefits in stride, never looking closely or consciously examining his gifts. Despite his wonderful resolution to keep notes and write a book of his great discovery he hadn't written a word.

His thoughts trailed to the Gogg and his problems. He could help just by speaking out. Should he? He had been and wanted to continue to be neutral. It would be different if he had a special feeling and a leaning in Dram's direction. But he hadn't. Or had he? He was stirred and encouraged by the charm of O Dram. In measuring the hours spent on Goggle in the company of pleasant women, however, credit went also to O Perceiver and Palpater.

Meanwhile I will devote to O Dram only that attention which will increase assimmolation," conceded Longfellow.

The Gogg expressed his gratitude. "Thank Sire. Forgive for not knock before enter."

Longfellow was disturbed next morning by a knock at the door. He was annoyed, and he allowed a moment to pass before he answered, his voice tingled with sharp edges of asperity.

"Yes? Who is it?"

The door was propelled open by Dram as he barged in without reply. His manner was both hurried and apologetic. His wife, lying next to Longfellow received a perfunctory, "Morning," then he went down on his knees alongside of Longfellow.

"Sire. Most terrible news compel to break in without wait."

He bowed and struck his forehead on the floor several times in self castigation over the need to violate Longfellow's sanctum. Holding his hands over his ears, he swung his head from side to side, for, however great his anguish over the news he carried, it required the physical help of his hands to make his head roll in sign of the full burden of his suffering.

Still on his knees, forehead resting upon the floor, the Gogg spoke. His voice was distant, resounding from the surface which was but an inch or two from his mouth and enclosed by the folds of his stomach and body. "Sire! Sire! Most terrible and foul thing happen on Goggle. Most terrible," a space of time intervened as his words took on the monotonous litany of prayer, "and foul. Most terrible and foul."

"Yes?" Longfellow prompted, not bothering to look over his shoulder.

"Sire. Lawsuit file in Logg by Goggler Astute, ask select cancel and new select start and," he let out a wail that moved up and down on the wailing scales, "most terrible and foul," the repetitious phrases separated the continuity of his words, "and Astute demand base for select be change or enlarge."

Nothing in that news should stimulate such excitement or fear and cause a violation of his privacy thought Longfellow. Gogg or no Gogg, host or no host, husband or no husband, he didn't like it.

But there was a little something extra he felt with O Dram, and to help her by helping the Gogg wouldn't harm O Perceiver or Palpater.

He didn't hear O Dram come into the room and walk up to him. As he turned, he found himself face to face with her. To prevent throwing her down with the momentum of his swing he had to hold her to him. As he did so, she kissed him gently—a very bold thing for a female on Goggle to do. When Longfellow did not berate her, but stood gazing into her eyes she closed them and said, "Thank, Sire."

He held her in his arms; he caressed and kissed her. The door slammed and he let go with a start.

Dram was at the door. "Beg pardon, Sire, if I be bold, this conduct," he twisted his hand at the wrist to indicate O Dram, "be improper. After all," his voice rose, his courage and sense of outrage reached fuller vent, "while it be wonderful, kind, and gracious thee permit be assimmolate, kiss mouth be pervert. Kindness of extend culture and civilize not same."

Longfellow could not find his voice for a moment. Oh life, he thought, there is a limit to clowning. Finally, he asked the Gogg. "Tell me what is considered perversion on Goggle?"

"Sire, it must be same in all place. What natural be permit. What not natural be pervert."

"And what is natural, and what is perverse?" inquired Longfellow.

"What natural nature permit. What cannot, be perverse." The explanation did not express the background of this kind of thinking, but Longfellow could visualize Peter One telling the Gogglers kissing was perverse because he did not like to waste time kissing or to kiss the hairy faces.

"Why do you consider it a perversion when I kiss O Dram on the mouth?"

"That rule. Pervert be interpret. Moral stricture. Goggler interpret rule as go along. Not for self, but for other, according what do or claim do."

"This rule of conduct is strange to me. I will think about it.

And, since the invasion exposed him lying in bed with this man's wife, he resented it. So his resentment operated to make him nasty and stubborn.

"Go down to the patio," he flung the words over his shoulder, "and I will see you there."

Thus reproved, Dram backed out on his hands and knees, dragging his head along the floor. Longfellow arose, and wearing his resentment outwardly, proceeded to bathe although he was angry enough to make Dram sweat for an hour. While he bathed his anger boiled and simmered. For these last few weeks he had conducted himself properly, refusing to join O Dram or any other woman in an act that violated proper religious conduct. Call it assimmolation or anything else, give approval, or even pray for it, to Longfellow it was adultery and sin and an act that would consign him to burn in Hell or suffer in purgatory. This time, weakening in his resolve, he had succumbed and committed the sin . . . and the Gogg had walked in to see him in bed with his wife. That the Gogg had not even winked at the congress which obviously joined O Dram and Longfellow so Longfellow could dissemble, was offensive to him, and he slashed at the water in his anger.

O Dram disappeared upon discovering his mood and Longfellow stomped down the stairs alone. There he joined the Gogg to find Perceiver, Upright, and Muddle with him. Their presence meant they knew where he had spent the night. Also it meant that the stimulant which so excited the Gogg was one that crossed the personal interests of all the powerful men of Goggle. Perceiver was an open champion of Pompos and one of his following, while Upright was one of the members of the Gogg's law firm and a leader in his selection campaign.

"Now," Longfellow's manner and voice demanded, "what has put you into such a dither?" The square seated chair he was led to just suited the high importance which he felt.

"Sire." The Gogg, always first with words, attempted an answer. "Astute sue in Logg for new base. Ask base for select be set to side, or enlarge."

This much he had already heard, when he hadn't wished to listen. This much told him nothing new.

113

"Astute, by petition, challenge most big be Gogg. Theory of he for Gogg be different . . . and thee power with Goggler end."

Sudden comprehension brought Longfellow's attention to the situation at hand. Anything which threatened his omnipotence was a threat indeed. To refuse assimmolation because it was sinful, was right . . . and his privilege. But to eliminate the demand by establishing different values, would make him of less importance and less sought after than the lowest caste of Gogglers. Like water flowing through clutching fingers, he saw his wealth and power slipping away from him. No longer could he, if he ever did so, choose on whom he would bestow assimmolation, or decide, if he ever did so, who deserved the greater, or added culture and civilization. The walls of the temple in which he was God would crumble like a house suffering a direct hit. But what could do this? What revolutionary theory—that had any merit at all—could do this? Elucidation was not long in coming.

"Astute argue," Upright tried to explain, "base for select be outdate. What do when Goggler animal not for present civilize. Most big be symbol of force and power. Must be right and reason which control. Therefore, say Astute, most big now urge for Gogg be symbol of what be before, whereas and wherefore, more sound foundation for choose and measure be what man have behind. Oh," Upright brushed aside further argument, "what use talk. Be ridiculous; be specieous; be not customtution; be . . . be . . . not what do want."

He clinched the argument against discussion. "Whole come out when matter argue before Logg. Why be disturb about what never happen? Logg sure deny fantastic theory."

The men all seemed to be in agreement and the Gogg accepted the general opinion. Before they left it was determined that Upright and Muddle would oppose the petition, and Pompos, as another candidate, would appear as a friend of the court urging that Astute's petition be denied. For the moment, the political enemies parted friends.

Court processes being rapid in Goggle, the Logg convened the very next day to hear this momentous case. Longfellow found that it would have been impossible to get into the Logg if he were any less an illustrious person, so large were the crowds trying to hear the proceedings. He was ushered to his seat in the front row, flanked by one for the Gogg and one for Perceiver. The Court was not yet in session, and the running talk between the Gogg and Perceiver made it clear that they had had another strategy meeting the night before and had decided there was nothing they need do and they would therefore do nothing except to carry out their agreement to have the opposition to the petition argued by Upright, Downright, Twaddle and Twiddle with Pompos, though a rival candidate of the Gogg, part of his camp on this issue urging against the petition as friend of the Court. "Friend of the Court" really meant one arguing in ones own interests.

While waiting for the Loggicers, Longfellow made a closer inspection of the courtroom. It had already impressed him with its austerity—due to the lofty stone ceilings and walls. A circular line guided the walls around the room and the light came from vault holes at odd breaks in the ceiling. The walls were ornamented with pictures of former Loggicers. Here too they hanged the office holders when they were ex. Some of the pictures showed the subjects wearing their masks. It was a curiosity which prompted him to ask Perceiver.

"How is it that some of the Loggicers wore their masks when their pictures were painted"?

Perceiver studied the pictures.

"Those thee do see wear mask did never get beyond mask stage. These die or resign before Gogg who appoint did lose incumbentcy. That mean, these did never look forward and, since painting be history of past Loggicer, these appear as actual."

The Clerk of the Court rapped for order and the Loggicers filed in. A murmur rose among those assembled in the court. Seven of the Loggicers were facing forward and six backward. The whispers reached Longfellow and his friends. No one had ever seen the Logg so broken up. On questions of law involving the incumbent Gogg who appointed the twelve Loggicers other than Popoff the twelve must face backwards and show their masks to the audience. On questions not involving a law of the Gogg, all thirteen were to look forward. There was therefore no basis for seven forward and six backward. The theory of the barristers, and one later shown to be correct, was that the twelve Dram appointees divided on whether this question was one which involved the incumbent Dram. Six thought it did and faced backward and six thought it did not and faced forward.

The barristers who were to argue filed in immediately afterward and placed their hands on the polished stone counsel table. Acting for Astute, the Gogg pointed out to Longfellow were barristers Sidle, and Judge Riddle. Popoff waved his hand, indicating that the fight was to begin. Sidle rose. His voice was stentorian and aggressive.

"Honor! Many century back when tribe small and leader need power to lead Goggler and fight and destroy enemy, Goggler take, or force take, most big in tribe as leader. Theory be follow 'til three-hundred year gone when Goggle be bless by Peter One."

Everybody, except Sidle and Riddle, looked around at Longfellow. The voice of Sidle continued.

"Peter One accept leader and define most big as not limit to who be most tall or most wide or other one dimension. Define most big as who do most for country; be virtual father of country. Peter One wisedom show live and govern be by right and reason, not force and seizin. Peter One bring assimmolate more great and grow culture and civilize. Through develop culture and civilize come emphasis on reason in select of Gogg, choose most big for benefit of most Goggler.

"Up to this far, be no conflict. Now," he pounded the counsel table and awakened several of the Loggicers, "if Gogg choose be Goggler for benefit of most great number, choose be base on consider of all fact. What in past guide we not be final if wisedome dictate other. Court and decision hold Goggler be Goggle-eyed. Once see thing and judge more big or more best, not can challenge choose. Be final."

"If Goggler use different base for decide than past, but use Goggle-eye and choose Astute with not regard of what be project as base for select, then choose be final, and must be accept."

"If Goggler peek in different place for judge, be right and choose final."

The speech of Sidle was so telling that the Court and the attorneys and proctors for the response became restless and their clothes rustled as they shifted in their seats. Upright poured water for himself from a pitcher that stood in the center of the table. Downright cautiously looked around at the Gogg, his eyes conveying his fear for the result. As Sidle sat down, Judge Riddle and Pompos rose. Pompos wanted to make the next address as friend of the court, but Riddle turned a sharp eye on him, pointed his finger at Pompos' seat, and after a fraction Pompos sat down again. Attention focussed on Riddle who was the only one of the counselors and judges who wore no hat.

Longfellow whispered out of the corner of his mouth, "Is there anything unusual about Judge Riddle not wearing a hat while all the others do?"

The Gogg answered, "Be permit no hat."

He would have gone into greater detail but Riddle had begun to talk and they didn't want to miss anything. He summed it up quickly, "Riddle once member of court; profoundest thinker. Not need keep head cover in presence of Logg and law."

The last phrase sounded like one of the Latin proverbs Longfellow had heard lawyers use back home. The harsh voice of the speaker cut into his hearing. It had a sharp tone as Riddle cracked his words out . . . as though by that process he would punish the listeners. It was not what he said that made an impression, it was the way he said it. His arms rose slowly with the rising innuendo of a long, meaningless sentence, and then he brought them down with a crash on the counsel table in front of him.

"That," he shouted in conjunction with the last table bang, "be tyranty—despoty—unadulterate despoty. Goggler creature of dignify—need be so treat. He who steal purse, steal purse, but he who rob vote—right participate in manage of self and Goggler and country"—he fumbled for the right word—"why, why, why—be indeed thief."

Riddle took a large silk handkerchief from his pocket, dusted off his seat and then wiped his head. Carefully he put the four corners of the handkerchief together between two fingers and flipped it forward so it snapped. Then taking the peak, which was the center of the handkerchief, he pushed it through the hole in his lapel. All this so held the attention of the Loggicers that they could not look to Upright and tell him to proceed. When Riddle was satisfied with the way his handkerchief lay, he looked up at Popoff, smiled an icy smile, and nodded as though his head was not firmly affixed and might fall off. One smile released the other. Popoff smiled, turned toward Upright and nodded to him.

"You talk."

Both Upright and Pompos stood up to talk. A sign from Popoff cast Pompos out of order and he smacked back down, his impatience adding violence to the process.

Upright, who had been waiting to go ahead, started. "Honor." As soon as he had said this, Pompos stood up, caught the stare of the Chief Judge and sat down.

"Honor." Upright turned to Longfellow. "Sire." He had ideas of help from Longfellow and showed him great deference.

The manner of Upright's presentation called for a proper interval of waiting before he launched into his principal argument.

"Petition must be deny. First, it challenge court while ask Court assist. Consider." He pronounced the word as if it had been made with apples. "Court establish under system of present Goggship. Petition challenge govern and ask court destroy govern. Consider more; all Loggicer on court appoint by Gogg select by customtution. Petition challenge Gogg who appoint Loggicer at same time accept Gogg by ask assist of Loggicer he appoint. No Honor, we not permit. Petition seek break unity of Goggler into many party. Differ class be, and this proper, for be way in Goggle for some century. But party? Disrupt unity and make inside strife. Make differ cult and differ worship? Blaspheme Peter," Upright pointed to Longfellow, "to say some worship what be before . . . and other worship what behind."

He paused, indignation reddening his eyes while the bristles of his neck and face stood as upright as his name.

"One more think, Honor, and close. As did say, create divide in Goggler, create disunion. Be end? Never. One grade back . . .

once release grasp on proper thing, then back fall be sure. Grant petition, divide Goggler once. Remain so? If permit divide once why not other party? If Goggler follow other base for culture and advance; seek assimmolate other way; what stop confuse? How plainass know which rule follow; get so drunk with notion and potion of base that, like all unthink follower, become drunk. Picture," Upright's face became sardonic, his voice scornful as he held his palm out in the direction of the Logg, "picture drunk unable determine which member bow to, or how make choose one or other. Problem of choose worship so confuse, these divide again many time 'til get to point where, drunk with worship of past, be not able determine which symbol of Gogg or party hold. Confuse on confuse, Gogg divide and redivide and Goggler lost."

Upright beat his breast, waved his arms and pounded the table, very much like his ancestors had done before him. "Must need be normal of life and able choose. Must choose normal base to choose. If Goggler not normal, then not vote normal, or decide normal."

Downright stood up as Upright sat down, the two working in such harmony that an observer might be misled into thinking they were working on a common spring.

"Honor! Learn brother advance many reason appeal to mind and emotion. Reason be reasoning. Develop one step at time, success of step prove point. But not give base of objection."

He stopped to mark his words so it would be understood that what came next was to be separated from what went before.

"Court have not jurisdiction in jurisprudent!"

It was a statement and a conclusion and a summation of everything Downright found important and potent. So impressed was Downright with the force and cogency of his opening charge that he slowly turned around, scrutinizing the Court, the Loggicers, the counsel, and the audience. When he was satisfied that everyone within hearing had had time to be impressed, he continued.

"In operate of govern, Gogg make all law . . . Logg interpret. Here in question of law, court must refuse petition and refer to Gogg who pass all law. No law say what form follow for majority of Goggler vote and only way to change present . . . only way make base of petition new base for select, be pass law. 'Til Goggler choose own method, or any method, petition have not stand in court."

Downright sat down. Again Pompos rose, ready to present his argument. His jumping up and down resembled a jack in the box. This so annoyed the Logg that now that it was properly Pompos' turn to address the court, he was waved aside by Coddle, one of the newer members of the court.

Pompos sat down. Together the five barristers stood up, executed a right turn and filed out of the room. The members of the Logg looked at one another and shrugged. Then they whispered. After a whispered consultation in which Fiddle leaned to Diddle and Diddle to Doddle and so on down the line, the whisperers settled back with Popoff. The barristers were recalled by the clerk and they rocked in as they had rocked out.

"Court," Popoff announced sadly, his face a melancholy gray, "not reach decide now. Consider and be back tomorrow."

The thirteen Loggicers all rose and shuffled out of the room. When Longfellow and the Gogg and the doctor-lawyer reached the hall outside, Upright was waiting for them. He hurried over, walking directly to Longfellow.

"Sire, have most great plea on behalf of self. Most first family on Goggle need honor of visit from thee."

The military bearing which characterized Upright gave him a magnificent stature and was very impressive. Longfellow hesitated. This was embarrassing for everybody. If he said no, it would be an affront . . . and an affront in the presence of many. If he said yes, Dram would no doubt go back and tell O Dram; and Perceiver would report to O Perceiver and Palpater. Longfellow had to learn to understand the great desire of all Gogglers to be assimmolated. He would like to visit and be friends with these people without suffering the tugs of demand and the disturbance of his belief and inhibition against indulging in adulterous conduct. Even an innocent visit would be misunderstood. A careful glance at Perceiver and Dram showed Longfellow that they were in intense consultation with one another and they might not know what he arranged with Upright.

"Why don't you call for me this evening and I'll join you for dinner?"

Upright's chin went in and his chest came out as he clicked his heels. His hand went to his head in salute.

"Thank Sire. Call six," He proudly rocked away energetically, and Longfellow joined the others. Seemingly, whatever had placed Dram and Perceiver in intense discussion a moment before was now settled, for there was no more to be said. The three of them walked along silently. At the entrance to the Gogg's house the Gogg asked Longfellow "Join we for dinner?"

"No, thank you, your Goggship. I want to think about what I heard today." replied Longfellow.

"Sire. Please to call."

Longfellow allowed his head to rise and fall a few times and he walked off with Perceiver. The doctor was possessed of a problem that kept him from speaking, and that condition satisfied Longfellow. He didn't feel like talking to the doctor-lawyer. When they reached the home of Perceiver, Longfellow kept walking to his own room.

Later, without being seen, he slipped out at six sharp to meet Upright. Upright greeted him joyously. "Sire, be proud night for we. Proud night history for Upright . . . great change in station."

Longfellow wondered for a second what he meant, but, having found such flowery phrase and emphasis laid on assimmolation he accepted that interpretation. At the same time he resolved that he would be upright even if Upright would not be. At Upright's house he was introduced to O Upright.

"Sire, permit to present O Upright."

The reason for great pride at the prospect of assimmolation became immediately apparent to Longfellow; he nodded from his Olympian importance. Although friendly and charming, the female was obviously half-caste. She looked rather slight to be the mate of the tall Upright, with delicate features matching her spare build. Not much else about her was attractive until she smiled and then her face lighted up. Longfellow warmed to her as though she were a child. From the moment he saw her smile, the irritation he had felt at his equivocal position passed and he began to enjoy his visit.

The outstanding sign of her half descent was neither on the grand side or the small side.

"Sire." The voice had a musical note and increased his interest, and when she curtsied it gracefully fitted her personality. While Upright and he went into the dining room, Longfellow noticed that O Upright saw to their places and their plates and their courses with a light, airy, prancing step that reminded him of a young and spirited mare. The dinner proceeded . . . Upright and Longfellow finding little to say and when they finished, Upright said.

"Sire, permit to show treasure. Many thing magnificent."

Longfellow disliked being offered the choice of gifts. He never hesitated to accept them when they were sent to him. In a brusque, offhanded manner, he told Upright, "If you wish to make me a gift, you choose it and send it over." With native shrewdness he added, "Your gift is your own conception of who you are. You are the judge of yourself. But I do not approve of and will not indulge in any sinful conduct. With that in mind you may do as you wish." In that way he said no in his mind to the evil of adultery without rejecting the good of giving . . and, for himself, of receiving. Though he performed no services it was customary for him to stay over. There was no wrongdoing in this and having grown tired and a little bored, Longfellow said, "Now Sir, will you show me the way?"

O Upright came tripping in to his room soon after he reached it. Such a small, delicate thing pleased him, and he speculated that he could lift her in his arms without any strain.

She was like a child, yet wise as any female, the combination of her qualities and features piqued him. Let the true Peterasses proclaim themselves great and this woman half-caste, to Longfellow she was one of the best. These thoughts riveted his attention on the obvious symbol of her sex which, due to lack of assimmolation, was only half the symbol it could be.

It would be interesting to find out at first hand why she did not affect being a full Peterass, by wearing one of those breastplates which hid the lack of culture. Although the false breast-plate really hid nothing, and the regular dress breastplate, which he had taught the Gogglers to call a gown, hid nothing also, there was a fine line between the two.

"O Upright," he made no effort to hide his curiosity, "other women of Goggle who are partly lacking in these evidences of culture," a gentle hand directed her to his reference, "wear the type of plate which has beauty and color and imitates a full culture. Why not you?"

"How?" There was no doubt about the puzzlement in her manner. "Be no way to set false over real."

That didn't work out as he understood it. He turned her face up. "If I understand correctly, women who have half the true culture," it was only necessary for him to apply slight pressure, "wear a type breastplate similar to those used by women who have no culture. The front bulges the natural form and covers what is there, at the same time it parodies the full evidence of culture, which they wish were there."

Shaking her head, she disagreed. "No. No. False breastplate be false and fashion be match body and personal. Female have one, find not match. Where be none, full bosom—two breast—design be put on."

"That would make it more difficult to tell the false from the true," he added.

"For some," said O Upright wisely, "most tell differ easy."

Back on earth he would say that a man didn't know a woman until he had lived with her. It required full and intimate knowledge to reach a goal which otherwise was an obstacle to seeing the real woman. Here it was the same. Friendship began after personal knowledge, so that interest couldn't be simulated or misinterpreted in the chase. O Upright was going to be one of his friends.

He was having breakfast the following morning when Upright marched in ceremoniously.

"Sire," he clicked his heels and bowed from the waist. "Logg prepare to give decision."

Longfellow pondered. He could wait and hear about the decision, although this was so momentous a situation that he probably should hear how the Logg handled it . . . Besides, if he were not there, he would be missed and it would cause gossip.

"Thanks for telling me." Yet he didn't want to appear at the Logg with Upright for the same reason that he didn't want to answer his invitation to visit, in front of others, yesterday.

"Suppose you go ahead. You are of counsel and will need more time to make your entrance. I'll be along in a short time—after I've had my breakfast."

Upright executed an about face with military precision and hurried out. A servant bustled her way around the room, generally relieving Longfellow of the necessity for any waste motion. Downstairs, when he was ready to leave, he turned O Upright's face to his. Because kissing was so strange to them he found special delight in it. It conveyed an affection which no other act could convey. He wanted to leave O Upright with a fond recollection of him.

Out in the streets the Goggler citizens hurried in the direction of the Logg. When they saw Longfellow they flip-flopped or genuflected or squatted, depending upon their class and sex. Some averted their eyes to avoid a show of servility. As at home, the greater number of Gogglers were from the lower castes, and this reminded him that higher class people were always in small numbers. Yet he reflected, his thought running ahead of him to the case at issue, the upper class had to depend upon the more numerous lower classes for a majority in numbers so they could rule. Democracy was a wonderful thing; and more wonderful still was the knowledge that the very conception of democracy came out of the brain of an animal like Peter Jenkins, one who lived a short life; and that an animal could have conceptions like democracy.

Before Longfellow could complete his meditations, he found himself walking through the corridors of the Logg.

At the door to the courtroom, attendants flipped and made way for him to return to his seat in the front row where the Gogg and the doctor were already seated. As he sat down, the curtain for the judges lifted. As before, seven were facing forward and six backward. The wizened clerk told the Sergeant-at-arms they were ready.

Each of the Barristers and Counselors stood before the well

or niche at which he had stood the day before. They simultaneously sat down. The whisperers, unable to confine their mouths, rattled them around and made noises. The signal to stop this was a clearing of his throat by Popoff. "Cchuh! Cchuh!"

The voice that followed was faltering, now and then struggling to enunciate a word.

"Petition of Goggle citizen, challenge system of select Gogg. Contend base for select be old fashion. Thus, say, not judge Goggler by future, by what he have before he, but more sound method and better govern be select and judge by past, by what he have behind. Revolutionary principle revolutionize whole system of select and govern if follow. Court hear argue and philosophy of leader of such argue. Be bombastic and noiseful . . . common and fustian . . . Be man who put out air. However disapprove of Goggler not can consider man in consider principle he advocate. Since Peter One, most big be unchallenge right of people of Gogg to determine. Doctrine most recent apply by Court unanimous in Matter of Pompos. Court point out Goggler have Goggle-eye . . . doctrine mean Goggler choose be final and absolute. Theory endorse fact that select be by measure and depend on eye. Not matter how test apply, be eye make final decision; Goggle-eye. Once decide, no argue of right or wrong. Same infirmity as people, Court not substitute opine for Goggle-eye.

"Not allow change in principle. Question here not challenge principle but affirm. Petition mean Goggle-eye be perfect and correct, but object of inspect and measure at present be not correct. Let Goggle-eye study what behind, not what before. Much to be seen in position. Past bear much on what leader will do.

"Not agree with ask Court direct Goggle people use what be behind. That eliminate future, what stand before. It stop say of Goggler which be better standard.

"Court feel petition ask too much. It seek destroy Goggle-eye principle. If Goggler see all candidate, study, look over, measure, determine by Goggle-eye which choose for Gogg, result be in principle. Look and test and measure, Goggler see both standard and select candidate who be most. Perhaps select he who have each quality yet not most of both. If Goggler do so, principle of Matter of Pompos apply and choose be final choose. Court allow Bombast party appeal to eye of Goggler for choose without eliminate present and past. Colleague Coddle, Diddle and Doddle join opine."

Longfellow, the Gogg and the doctor-lawyer looked at one another with curiosity. While the opinion showed that the petition was granted, and the past was to be presented to Gogglers as a basis for selection, there were only four votes accounted for out of an apparent looking forward seven. Before they could start to whisper and ask questions, the voice of Fiddle assumed the speaker's role. It was a clearer and steadier voice, though the Loggicer trembled as he handled his gavel and his jaws quivered like hanging drapes.

"Not disagree with Chief Judge. Result be right. Argue by Astute that new way for select be most progress and old method be old fashion, and must be declare not legal, be specious. Urge that Goggler choose best base for select and in same urge that Goggler be stop from old rule, be vice. Such principle urge dictate from Court and say select by democrazic standard. Astute manner be bombast, pomposity, despoty, brag, be attempt arrogate to self more great culture than true culture and show he be bold and tyranty. If he Gogg, be trouble for Goggle. But be not for Court tell Goggler how govern self. Democrazic principle urge by petitioner for self advantage, not be ignore because lose benefit of good quality. Matter of Pompos mean for Gogglers act democrazic. For Goggler choose Gogg, and, in choose, use method select which have most great appeal. If Bombast so befog Goggler these select candidate of Bombast, so it be. Peter help Goggle if these win."

There was a pause between the speeches while the courtroom audience and the barristers became restless. All five of the orators at the counsel table looked around triumphantly, for in effect each had won a victory. Both camps could present their ideas and theories to the Gogglers and so neither had been foreclosed. Everyone knew what the result was, after the first rustlings of restlessness, and all sat back to hear the minority opinion which would have no effect on the result.

Piddle addressed the acoustical board on the wall behind his seat. It was hard to tell that the face in the front of the mask was not delivering the opinion since the movements of the head under the mask made its motion seem real. Only the echoing voice destroyed the illusion. It was a hesitant and undecided voice which presented the minority opinion.

"Speak for self. Study petition careful; argue theory with brother; do much study and talk on subject. Agree principle of Matter of Pompos. Be base on customtution. Same reason Goggle-eye be final, omniscient, omnipotent . . . do hold eye must use in customtution sense. Perverse of justice say be customtution and avoid at same time customtution rule. If apply Goggle-eye rule, must use base which always use for test Goggle-eye. New theory have not place in govern. Petition should be reject and Goggle go on course develope by history, tradition and custom. Feel too, mention of Peter at same time tear down principle of descendants, and be blaspheme. Condemn such."

The audience sat back patiently and courteously. It was only decent to listen to these Judges who wanted to disagree. The followers of the Bombast cult however, were not interested in the proceedings and though they had enough respect for the Logg to sit and wait for the dissenting opinions, they couldn't restrain their conversations. Finally, Doodle being ready to speak his piece, the clerk rapped a gavel on the post. It gave off a solid ring, like a product which contained stone. The whispers died down. Doodle began, the monotone of his voice accentuated by the acoustical gymnastics.

"Much be said about Goggle-eye ascendant. Matter of Pompos support argue. No one dispute hold of case. Final and absolute. Only have not to do with matter in hand. Question be not of Goggle-eye, but Democrazy. Basic. We be Democrazy. Advocate, preach, follow, demand, pronounce, seek . . . er, choose . . . er, er, and follow, Democrazic principle. Be propose to change Democrazic? And be Democrazic to change?"

"What be Democrazy? Manage of govern by Goggler. Choose by Goggler of govern. Be present system Democrazy? Indubitable! If present system be Democrazic, other system, which be differ, not be. That be what petition seek. If change standard principle then tear down system. Tear down be not retain and change. Be destroy. Feel Democrazic practice we already use, and alway use, be true Democrazy. New method of operate destroy Democrazy. Petition seek to destroy whole structure of living and govern and break down erection of three-hundred year. Warn Goggler; warn everybody; if majority lead to Bombast— then dictator, tyranty and end of all we be stand for."

Upon the rendition of this final opinion, the barristers rose, right-faced, and marched out. The Loggicers were more solemn going out than they had been coming in. When the door closed behind them the audience filtered out.

It was several days before Longfellow heard any more about the new approach to selection, and then it was on a visit he made after a messenger advised that O Dram wished to see him. The delight with which he called upon her changed to curiosity that she had asked for him to call. His visits with her had been confined to the Gogg's house.

After they had spent a satisfying two hours and had a substantial lunch, O Dram asked, "Sire. Be good friend. Gogg occupy with campaign suggest thee like see Astute and study." As she said this, she leaned forward confidentially, although no one else was present in the room. "Gogg ask I be with thee when go to meeting of Astute. Will go?"

The idea intrigued him. He had thought of the campaign and the sophistry in regards to the various arguments and positions but he hestiated to ask O Dram where the meetings were held; and he feared his attendance might disrupt them . . . or even be misinterpreted; for those Gogglers who attended the Bombast meetings were those who agreed with the Bombasts, and those who attended the Goggs' or Pompos' meetings leaned to those candidates.

"All right," he agreed. "It's a good idea. Let us see what developments take place. We'll listen and watch. Let us go to a few meetings this week. When will the Bombasts hold their next meeting?"

"This night."

"Tonight? Then let us go and listen. I would like to see them and hear them."

"At least smell be good," O Dram added with pleasant anticipation.

Longfellow looked at her, uncertain whether the pleasant anticipation in her face really portrayed her feelings about the atmosphere of the Bombasts. Could it be that the Gogglers enjoyed the horrible smell which they exuded? The idea was absurd but he asked O Dram, "Doesn't the odor which the Bombasts give off offend you? Or the crowd?"

"Offend?" O Dram asked. "Why offend? Be odor of we and odor of we be perfume Goggler like. Be other odor different?"

Longfellow studied her a moment. The idea was droll to him, but he realized that in reality taste and feeling and smell were highly personal things. Even the civilized olfactometers with which he had come in contact reacted to the cheap perfume that some persons preferred, as well as to the very delicate perfume used by others. There were people he knew who could stand no perfume at all and many were the wrinkling of the noses he had observed when the so-called sweet smells were in the atmosphere. Animals who were famous for the sensitivity of their olfactories and could follow a scent for miles seemed to enjoy their own odor. Again he asked himself, what is good and what is bad? Some people like a rough touch, some a soft; some people like a hot chili that burns their tongue and guts, and others prefer a bland food that the chili eaters would consider tasteless. What was right on any given avenue was established by what the majority on that avenue did. If there were countries, and he had visited such, where the majority insisted on spiced foods, why could there not be countries where the majority insisted on air which had muscles? Perhaps his whole outlook was wrong. If the majority could determine what was normal in sight, smell, touch and taste, then it was perfectly reasonable that the majority would determine what was normal in their sex and other physical relationships. The Gogglers were giving him a course in reorientation.

The fact was, he thought, that in any body politic the majority determined each standard. Sometimes it took a bit longer for the majority view to crystalize, and when crystalized, to take hold. But over the long stretch, the majority opinion ruled. These ruminations had the effect of making him regurgitate his sanctimonious views on sex. The majority of persons in his country, holding a religious point of view which the Gogglers knew nothing of, believed, as Longfellow believed, that any sex relationship must be surrounded by the sacrament of marriage. Adultery was one of the great sins. But here, where Peter One had instilled his selfish and peculiar views, those views were the views of the majority. And perhaps this made them right or at least accepted. He must, in the reflection of this new light, reorient the angle of his thinking.

With a partial yielding to a flexible future, he turned to O Dram, "When and where will this meeting be held?"

"Must soon go or be too late," she answered.

He got up reluctantly, raised O Dram so they were both standing, then took her in his arms and kissed her.

O Dram said, "We go?"

Longfellow let her go. "Yes. Yes. Where will this meeting be held?"

"Main circle on Goggle where politic hold meet all time. Tonight Bombast meet big." She tugged at him. "Come." He released her grip on him and they started toward the exit.

An hour later they arrived at the big circle. As they approached they were discovered by the crowd and a cheer went up. The Gogglers registered their respect in the usual manner. Longfellow looked around to see great crowds milling about with lights suffusing the field. Arranging chairs formed a circle, the rows running in whorls similar to those in the street paving. Up in what appeared to Longfellow to be the front, a huge platform bore an enormous sign showing the face of Astute, the candidate of the Bombasts. The buttonhole eyes common to the Gogglers were, in Astute's case, tighter and smaller. The head and face were thinner, and a forelock of hair drooped over his right eye. Unlike the greatest majority, who had such flat nostrils they seemed to have no nose at all, Astute had a clearly defined hook nose.

When the seats were filled and the noisy crowd had grown impatient, a group of men filed onto the platform, led by Astute. Longfellow noticed he was taller and thinner than the others. He combed his hair with his fingers but the forelock kept falling in his face. He raised his hand before him, holding it at an angle and most of the noise stopped. Then he walked over to a seat and the next in file moved forward to address the Goggler crowd. This beefy aide faced out into the audience as if he could see them.

His chin was slung out under his broad square face emphasizing the jaw and hiding any neck. The hips, just as wide as the shoulders, made him look like a packed cubic sac. As he rocked from side to side on short bandy legs, like a well-stuffed balancing figure, he played a symphony of sound and wind—belching, grunting, puffing and exploding. His was the job of introducing Astute and, in all the noisy eruption he bellowed "Astute." Astute came forward, half smiling as he started to perform and the noise was stilled entirely.

"Goggler! Tonight make history." His strident voice came in yelps. "For many year, since begin time, we select Gogg by old front measure. Tonight know old select of front be old evil. Tonight explode old hold theory. Tonight!" He took a stance half bent over, erupted flatulently and then straightened up sharply.

"Consider! For many year select Gogg on base of what before without to know what behind." His yelping, added to his dialect, made him difficult to understand.

"Know we how Goggler be by what before and not yet test? Who know what length Goggler go, when use future as base for measure? We no know! Even select Gogg not tell how much count in future!

"When Dram first rise all patriot stand. These watch future with Gogg. Pompos too." At this point, applause and shouting from the audience drowned out his voice and he stopped, looking to right and left for approval. The noise quieted again. "Now Pompos want be Gogg. Great Pompos not new and Goggler need thing new. Need candidate with broad understand to carry Goggle through hard time. What new? What? What Goggler have behind! Proper base for measure and judge be look behind Goggler see how carry self; how shape past; and judge what future. Past carry what shape tomorrow. Word of before be hear in song of after. Then Goggler who sound powerful before select, not change after select. No deep baritone change to falsetto. For see Goggle grow from past, need select Astute as Gogg!"

Slapping his buttocks to a tune sounded from a gaseous release, and marching with his shifting carriage from one end of the platform to the other, he stirred the crowd until, like a large beast, it shrieked, whistled, stamped and hooted. Astute stood on the platform, his face, framed by his hair like an overturned centipede, beaming and scowling. Longfellow had the impression that the crowd did not know whether they approved or disapproved; they just continued to cheer and howl. Finally, the noise died down and Astute was able to resume.

"Candidate be judge not only by Bombast, but by high and low skill and imagine. I give first, and most great Bombast for Gogg, Astute!"

This time as he marched up and down the platform, he was followed by his political supporters. Suddenly he stepped up to the front again, smiled, turned, and bowed to each section of the audience, slowly completing the circle, punctuating each bow with a full expression as a prophesy of the future.

Completing the circle of bowing, he stood and waited for the noise to abate, his eyes opening and closing slowly, sly and subtle like. The noise continued and a loud explosion was heard in the right section of the audience; then the same in the center; then on the left. It took a few moments before the crowd and Longfellow realized that these were ventriloquial effects produced by Astute himself. When the crowd realized it, they began to laugh, jumping up and down with delight, encouraging the explosive effects to continue. Entertained by Astute's performance, the crowd finally became weary from the waves of laughter that rolled through and over them, and relaxed to listen. Astute was able to continue.

"On what Goggler rest claim? What not see? Or, if see, useful of which be guess? No! What Goggler have behind be ready see. Be deep, wide, broad . . . and not all for see!"

Again he bowed, a prodigious bow for all the audience, and,

Slapping his buttocks to a tune sounded from a gaseous release, and marching with his shifting carriage from one end of the platform to the other, he stirred the crowd until, like a large beast, it shrieked, whistled, stamped and hooted.

as he retired to his seat, the audience sat drinking in the so-called perfume which permeated the air. Longfellow felt stifled, and wanted to get away, but O Dram, like the other Gogglers, acted as though the aroma was pleasant. All around him, Longfellow saw that the crowd sat in a partial hypnosis. Longfellow pulled and pushed O Dram to get away. Finally he could breathe again. By the time they were back at the Gogg's cave, criers in the streets were proclaiming the new party's platform.

Longfellow pondered. There are more turns and devolutions in man's efforts to govern himself than most people know. Perhaps because of the very confusion of new things, new thoughts and new approaches, people cling to the standards and principles for which their fathers and forefathers have always stood.

The result of the court hearing was really of no significance, thought Longfellow. Whether the radicals of Peter One had won out and these were their descendants, or whether the conservatives of Peter One had won out and these were their descendants, did not matter. These were Peter One's people . . . his children. Whatever their proclivities, these were his.

Thus engaged in thought Longfellow walked into the patio with O Dram where the Gogg awaited them. The Gogg's grotesquely absurd, anthropoid face asked Longfellow what he thought; the question which he did not speak was presented by screwing his face into contours.

After a long silence, Longfellow told him. "To those who respect the past, Astute and his antics are ridiculous. Those who seek something different, what exactly they don't know but look to discover, may find him intriguing . . . . Suppose a Goggler were discovered who had the superlative in the espoused bases for selection. Bigger in every measure than yourself or Pompos; more Bombast than Astute. Would all candidates withdraw in his favor?"

"Certain not. Not candidate but party leader decide each party stand for what emblem stand. Goggler who have other quality not be true Gogg. Not have true belief when believe in other too. Party must ignore."

Longfellow nodded. "I suppose there is that to be said. Probably most anyone could fill the job equally well, regardless of the basis on which they were selected." He had hardly finished expressing this thought, when he realized the Gogg might be affronted; the Gogg's gape showed he was right.

"Not that that applies to you of course. I said most anyone. You are exceptional."

The soothing syrup having smiled the Gogg, Longfellow looked at the outside darkness and told them, "I must be leaving for home." He asked O Dram, "When do we go again?"

"Tomorrow if wish," she replied.

That week Longfellow and O Dram went to two more meetings; one of them was for Pompos.

After the second meeting, on the way home, O Dram was rather quiet and Longfellow could tell something was on her mind. At her home she asked him to come in and have a drink with her. Once inside she prepared the drinks, and when he was comfortable she sat in a chair facing his.

"Thee desire do thing for I . . . that which not do for other?" She hitched her chair closer to his.

The quaint look which greeted her did not dispute her claim to his special friendship and consideration.

"Throw self at feet for favor." Suiting the words, she got down on her knees with her breasts waving at him; she looked up in supplication.

"What do you want me to do?" he asked.

Avoiding a direct statement of her wishes, she told him, "I be woman of Gogg, first Lady Goggle. This mean all to I." Her sagacity dictated flattery. "Til thee come, be only life to I. Still be second most important."

The exact direction of her words escaped him and he wondered. "I still say, what do you want me to do?"

"Thee have Dram reselect as Gogg."

"And how would you suggest I do that?"

"Not know. Thee be Peter. Thee know all. Goggler do as thee say. Talk Gogg."

"Does he know that you are asking this of me?"

The reply was slow in coming. "Yes."

"Very well. I'll do whatever I can."

"Oh thank thee, Sire."

He took her by the hand and stood up, lifting her off her knees. With his free hand he pushed her breasts back to the breastplate. "We'll talk later."

Sitting around after dinner, Longfellow asked the Gogg, "You feel that you will not be reselected?"

"As stand, no. Pompos split vote, and win of Astute be in air."

"What can I do that would help your reselection?"

"Sire. Thee be Peter. Need only rule from Peter that Democrazic principle eliminate Bombast party."

"Eliminate them? The Logg has ruled they cannot be eliminated; they are entitled to be heard by the Gogglers and only the Gogglers may reject them."

"Alternate plan be to hold confer with all candidate, tell thee take over as Gogg, and select be over."

"But how will my taking over make you remain in office?"

"As Peter Two, thee appoint I Chief, and I continue as Chief. I not introduce new law. Only Gogg do."

Longfellow glanced at O Dram's face and watched the imploring look return. A fleeting memory of the day when the Gogg objected to his kissing her skidded through his mind. Everything would be changed if he accepted. Once he took over, like Peter One, he could make new laws and rules. It would be fun trying to improve on that masterful kibitzer's kidding . . . . But no, he didn't like the idea at all. The Gogg would have . . . should have to stand by himself. Perhaps, he thought, if he announced he was going to vote for Dram that would help. His growing reluctance had been anticipated by Dram and O Dram; the Gogg suddenly recalled something he had to do.

"Sire forgive. I go. O Dram stay." He walked off in his rocking gait, arms hanging below his knees.

For a few moments after he had gone, Longfellow and O Dram sat there saying nothing. Then O Dram took Longfellow by the hand and led him to the bedroom which they now occupied when he stayed at the Gogg's house.

Lying in bed caressing O Dram like a true voluptuary tasting the bed delights of her body, stirred the thought that if Dram lost the election, things might be different. But he knew he couldn't interfere with the democratic process on Goggle. It had taken generations for these Goggle-people to advance to where they were and if he injected himself and took over, it would be an act of dictatorship which he had been taught to abhor . . . even more than immoral assimmolation. His discomfort touched a chord in his mind. Perhaps, he reasoned, if he yielded somewhat in his absolute insistence on these other moral proprieties he might be able to hold fast to his principles on the question of democracy. After all, the code of sexual conduct between man and woman could have been established by man. Perhaps the Ten Commandments did not come from God. Adultery might turn out to be what man defined it to be. Adultery was voluntary sexual intercourse with a married person by one other than the spouse. What was a spouse? Marriage on Goggle was not the same as on earth. And if he consented to these people's requests he would be advancing the breed of the Gogglers; developing them; cultivating their best qualities. Darwin had pointed out that life was a survival of the fittest and he, Peter Longfellow, would be advancing the Gogglers' fitness. Would that be enough? He chucked O Dram under the breasts as he would a child under the chin.

"Suppose," he asked himself out loud, "I agreed to assimmolate the Gogglers if they selected Dram for Gogg? Would they vote for Dram?"

O Dram's face became a caricature of delight. "This be sure Sire."

"And you would not mind?"

"How mind when thee do for I?"

"All right. We will announce that I will assimmolate all Gogglers if they vote for Dram."

O Dram kissed and caressed his body as if she would eat him. This was her way of telling him how pleased she was. Forgotten in the pleasure of her conduct was the thought that he might be corrupting the ballot by this form of payment; or that he might be lowering his morals by enjoying the sacrifice.

"That be absolute true," the Gogg was saying. Several days had gone by since Longfellow had agreed to assimmolate the Gogglers and the agreement had been publicly announced. The Gogg could no longer restrain his promptings that Longfellow make arrangements for direct service to Pompos and Astute. It was not enough to influence the Gogglers. Dram wanted to wrap it up completely by getting the two candidates to withdraw and he argued and urged that Longfellow's services be offered directly to Pompos and Astute. Longfellow, familiar with the political practices on earth, thought that if Pompos and Astute were offered important offices they could be sounded on complete withdrawal. Especially was this the case, Longfellow pointed out, since they were going to lose anyway.

"That show," said the Gogg "that thy experience and more great intelligence give Goggle new advance. Know where change be to advantage of Goggler."

"Yes," admitted Longfellow grudgingly.

"Then must act. Tell Pompos and Astute thee assimmolate family and arrange important office in govern."

Longfellow acquiesced. "All right. Make an appointment for me here in which you, Pompos, and Astute will be present. Make it for tomorrow."

In this situation he would not lose the whip. It would not be a once-done, completely-done act, but he would be in control. Returning to his thoughts while the Gogg hurried to arrange the appointments, Longfellow recalled the exigencies of history. That projected diary of his wherein the story of Goggle would be recorded must be started at once—today. This was the real beginning . . . becoming spiritual and physical adviser to the Goggle families in their search for culture and assimmolation. He took out the sheets he had prepared and then halted with pen poised over paper while he debated an idea. Since he was almost a God . . . he paused at the thought . . . for one became a god when people worshipped one as such, the right time to start would be the following day, after his meeting, and the perfection of the plan to assure succession for the Gogg. Yes, that was the time to start. He cut a number of pens, sure that he would need many for the writing he would do the next day.

Bedtime found him well pleased with the plans for the morrow. Unconsciously, he breathed deeper and deeper until his chest expanded beyond any previous development.

The next day he had barely finished his breakfast when the Gogg appeared. "Sire. Arrangement be make. Pompos and Astute be here in short."

Longfellow inclined his head. It would not be long now. While they were talking, Astute and Pompos were announced. Longfellow told a servant to take Astute into the next room. Then he asked Dram again, "You feel certain that they wish me to assimmolate their families?"

"Positive Sire. To do other be most great heresy, sacrilege and blaspheme. For sake of make sure these withdraw, tell each of important position in govern. Pompos like be Chief Justice."

"Won't Astute object if he wants the position?"

"Thee be master of govern and not make offer when together. Essence of good govern be talk separate — confidential. While other not witness." His hand waved to cast a slight on his own abilities and thinking, "I not tell Peter what do."

Longfellow allowed his eyes to rest upon the Gogg, while he took stock. Some government men did just the contrary, insisting on witnesses. Why, he pondered?

The Gogg hustled Pompos into the room.

"Sire." Pompos bowed obediently, "I call at request. What do?"

Longfellow contemplated the fat certainty of the man in the light of what he had to tell him and in the shadow of Pompos' obvious sycophancy.

"Pompos. As one of the great leaders of Goggle, I felt it was fair to discuss with you the government of Goggle."

Pompos looked at him wide-eyed.

"I know that I have promised assimmolation to the Gogglers, but someone as important as yourself should be among the first," Longfellow continued. "But aside from that, I must rely upon you to help manage this State as it should be managed. I need your word that when a vacancy for Chief Judge of the Logg occurs, you will accept."

Pompos' stare changed to a smile and spread to a grin. Speechless he nodded his head in assent.

"The Gogg will need any reports or suggestions you can make —and right now he needs your advice and counsel on how to promulgate this projected ascendancy."

"Sire." Pompos bent down and kissed Longfellow's finger. Then he looked in the direction where Astute had vanished. "Need be appease. Follower of self not problem. Announce and these mad with delight." He stared after Astute again. "But Astute not understand, Sire. Let be State Barrister and satisfy."

Longfellow was relieved. The whole thing was working out exactly as planned. There was little surrender of moral principles here since moral principles were really man made. His superiority in all phases of living and intellectuality made it a duty for him to devote himself to the uplifting of the Goggler's standards. No one could criticize him for following a plan which inevitably would improve these people. He allowed Pompos to go while he went back to his desk.

At that moment Astute came in, respectfully bowing with arms swinging. The Gogg went out to Pompos. Astute showed his respect for Longfellow by remaining at the door. This gave Longfellow an opportunity to look him over. His cuirass and breastplate were carelessly worn and the thin face showed cunning. Longfellow thought of Shakespeare's line, "Yon Cassius hath a lean and hungry look."

"You have heard that I will assimmolate the people if the Gogg will be reselected?" he began.

Astute nodded, his body still bending in the middle, his manner that of one who waits. Longfellow continued, "I will assimmolate your family if you wish."

Astute remained bent in the middle, his hands swinging below his knees, his forelock hung over his eyes. There was uncertainty in the manner in which he spoke. "Thank Sire. But this I not wish."

Longfellow was not certain he had heard the man correctly

and, like a diver who has launched himself only to see too late there is no water in the pool, he could not stop what he had planned to say.

"And since there will be no contest for Gogg, and I consider your services very valuable, I have suggested to the Gogg that you be appointed State Barrister."

Astute's eyes opened wide, but he remained standing where he was. "Thank Sire. But I do not wish family assimmolate; and do not wish be State Barrister."

Longfellow drew back. He heard, but at the same time, because the reply had not been contemplated, he did not hear. When, after several seconds, the rejection had registered, he asked. "You do not wish to have me assimmolate your family?"

Astute shook his head in the negative and his forelock waved from side to side.

Still incredulous Longfellow inquired again. "And you do not wish to be State Barrister?"

Astute still waved his negative. "I wish to do this myself. I wish to be sire of own family—to make own tribe—maybe own party."

"Your own party? You mean you will not withdraw from the campaign for Gogg."

Astute stopped waving his head. "Not wish to stop, but follower all stop. This campaign over, but I make own party, and own family and when party grow—make new campaign so I be Gogg and have own people and country!"

With the last words Astute moved, a devilish grin on his face. Without looking back at Longfellow, he rolled from side to side in an expression of cockiness and left.

While it came as a complete surprise to Longfellow that Astute should reject his offer, Longfellow knew that Astute was a minor minority now that Longfellow had agreed to assimmolate all the Gogglers.

Nonetheless, Longfellow sat there thoughtfully for a few minutes. He took up his pen. Of course, what he wrote was intended for the future, and the people he knew—all those on earth, reading his report, would condemn his departure from their moral principles. But, and here he meditated deeply, why should he write for the people on earth? This was Goggle—and he—Peter Longfellow . . . King. In fact . . . his dark eyes rolled upward and his dark countenance focussed them even more upward . . . he was like a God to them. He was Peter Two, a fact he now admitted, which made him a God. Being a God, he had no need to write and instruct simple humanity. They could and would worship his godliness and find many reasons why his conduct here was godly— even holy. If he wrote and tried to explain, it would only confuse them. Each man was entitled to his beliefs and if some found his conduct holy and others only righteous and still others as a benediction to benefit and guide his children, that was as it should be.

To Hell with that, he thought, and tossed down his pen, uncertain whether he was consigning the idea, and the pen, to the Hell he knew on earth, or the Hell which was the other side of his new Heaven, where he was God.